MAULIK PANCHOLY

BALZER + BRAY
An Imprint of HarperCollins*Publishers*

Also by Maulik Pancholy
The Best at It

Balzer + Bray is an imprint of HarperCollins Publishers.

Nikhil Out Loud
Copyright © 2022 by Maulik Pancholy
All rights reserved. Printed in the United States of America.
No part of this book may be used or reproduced in any manner
whatsoever without written permission except in the case of
brief quotations embodied in critical articles and reviews. For
information address HarperCollins Children's Books, a division of
HarperCollins Publishers, 195 Broadway, New York, NY 10007.
www.harpercollinschildrens.com

Library of Congress Control Number: 2022938131
ISBN 978-0-06-309192-4

Typography by Carla Weise
22 23 24 25 26   PC/LSCH   10 9 8 7 6 5 4 3 2 1
❖
First Edition

For Mom,
who teaches me courage

CHAPTER 1

It feels more like a rock concert than an awards show out there. The sound of all the screaming fans in the auditorium makes the entire backstage area vibrate. There must be ten thousand kids in those seats.

I peek through the curtains to try to get a glimpse, but the glare of the spotlights rotating back and forth makes it impossible to see.

A hand squeezes my shoulder, and I spin around.

"Feeling good, Nikhil?" Josh has to shout over all the noise to be heard. His tight-fitting gray blazer, dirty blond hair, and the tanned white skin of his cheeks glow purple under the dim backstage lights.

"Pretty good?" I smile. Josh is the head producer on *Raj Reddy in Outer Space*. And at the moment, I have a feeling he's just as nervous as I am. Even though we already know I'm winning tonight, this is still work. *RROS* is the number-one animated kids' series on TV right now, and it's Josh's job to make sure it stays that way.

"Five minutes until you're on stage!" a wiry guy wearing a headset and dressed in black from head to toe barks at us as he scurries by. Adrenaline courses through my body, making my fingers tingle. The headset guy is just about to turn the corner when he looks back at me. He covers the microphone dangling in front of his mouth. "Sorry to geek out, but I'm a huge fan! You're awesome!"

He lingers for a second, waiting for me to respond. I'm not quite sure what to say, so I give him a thumbs-up, hoping he doesn't notice that my thumb is shaking.

Josh hands me a smartphone enclosed in a plastic underwater protective case. "Remember we're grabbing this whole thing to play on social media, so be sure to record some stuff backstage and take some video of the audience. And at the end of your speech, wave at the camera and give us your signature line right before it all pours down on you, okay? Have fun out there. Just be yourself!"

Mom bends down in front of me. She gently tugs the bottom of my T-shirt, smoothing it out. "You've got this! Even if you're dressed like someone kidnapped my actual son and replaced him with a member of a boy band."

I look down at my T-shirt. It's extra long with a rounded hem, and the logo of *Raj Reddy in Outer Space* is emblazoned across the front of it. My black jeans are super tight, and my feet are shoved into a pair of white high-tops.

These are *not* my regular clothes.

I grab an imaginary air mic and deadpan at Mom. "*Should* I join a boy band?"

She laughs so hard I can see her back molars. "Maybe stick to the voice acting for now, okay?" She reaches out to ruffle my hair, but before she can, Josh swoops in and ushers us closer to the entrance.

A rush of anxiety floods my body. My mouth goes dry, and my lips feel chapped.

From where we're standing, I can see the entire stage and almost all of the audience. The auditorium is massive. I turn on the phone and hit the Record button. "Hey, everyone! We're backstage at the Kids'

Cartoon Awards!" I do my best to sound more confident than I feel. "Check this out!" I smile at the camera and then flip the phone around to capture the spotlights sweeping back and forth across the heads of the audience. Onstage, two Jumbotrons flash bright white and then fade to black. A clip of *Raj Reddy in Outer Space* starts rolling. "There I am!" I spin the phone toward the Jumbotrons. A cartoon version of me is strapping on a jetpack and staring up at a dark night sky filled with hundreds of stars. You can just make out the glowing edge of the moon and hints of colorful planets in the distance. The offscreen voice of Intergalactic Commander Regina Marks—played by my favorite costar, Faraja Mwangi—slices through the silence. "Raj, you'll be given the details of your assignment as soon you land on the planet Pacura. But before you go, I have just one question for you." There's a pause, and then the whole audience screams Commander Marks's famous catchphrase in unison: *"Are you ready, Reddy?"*

The screen cuts to a close-up of my cartoon face. The rockets on the jetpack ignite. I raise my watch to my lips and whisper into it, "Oh, I'm ready, Commander. *I'm Raj Reddy.*"

The audience goes wild. The deep bass of an

announcer's voice booms through the sound system. "You love him as the voice of undercover, intergalactic kid detective Raj Reddy! Please welcome this year's winner for Best Voice Actor on an Animated Television Series . . . Nikhil Shah!"

Josh practically pushes me onto the stage. I turn back to glance at Mom. She's pumping her fist at me. Then, I look directly at the audience. My eyes go wide. I can see all the way up to the very last row now. There are even more people out here than I thought. My right leg starts to tremble, so I do a little dance move to try to hide it. I spin around on the heels of my high-tops. The audience roars. I throw both my arms up in the air, and they leap to their feet. I walk up to the podium. A glass trophy is sitting on top, waiting for me. It gleams under all the stage lights.

I lower the mic. Thousands of hands wave "hello" at the camera on my phone.

"Um . . ." I feel sweat beads forming along my brow. "Thank you. Uh . . . I wanna thank . . ."

I practiced my speech at home, but now it feels like all the words have flown out of my brain.

"Well, I want to thank all the fans . . . of course!" A huge cheer goes up in the audience. "And . . . oh yeah, my mom! And . . . our producer Josh . . ."

My voice bounces back at me through the stacks of speakers flanking the stage. It echoes around the auditorium.

It's strange to hear my *own* voice, so loud, right after watching that video clip. When I play Raj Reddy, I pitch it up a little to add a hint of character.

I glance at the frozen frame of Raj on the Jumbotron, whispering into his watch.

The resemblance is uncanny. I mean, he's obviously a cartoon character. And our faces aren't actually that much alike. But he's Indian American, and I'm Indian American. We're both skinny. And we're both pretty tall for our age.

"Speech! Speech! Speech! Speech!" the audience is chanting. I feel my cheeks turn red. What else did I want to say? Out of the corner of my eye, I see Josh reminding me to keep taking video. I turn the phone toward my face.

I grin, pitch my voice up, and say, "I'm Raj Reddy!"

Right on cue, what feels like three tons of green goo comes showering down on me.

CHAPTER 2

As soon as I'm offstage, the wiry headset guy guides us down the hallway to my dressing room. He looks me over. "Nice work, dude! They loved you out there!"

He unlocks the door to let Josh, Mom, and me in, whispering under his breath, "You know, the more goo you get, the bigger the star you are! Again, huge fan!" Then he hands Josh my trophy and disappears down the hall.

The three of us burst out laughing.

"Hey, was my speech okay—?" I start to ask as we walk in. But Streak, my dog, bounds out of his bed, where he's been waiting for us this whole time. He darts straight toward me, yipping with excitement. Mom intercepts him, and he covers her face in sloppy, wet kisses, trying his best to wriggle out of her arms.

"I don't want that green stuff all over the dog!" Mom holds him tight. She shuts the dressing room door behind her. "Go shower in the bathroom. Josh and I will wait out here!"

There's a knock, and headset guy pops his head back in. "Someone named Anton is at the stage door? With his mom. Can I send them in?"

"Yes!" My whole face lights up.

Anton is hands down my best friend in the entire world. We've been inseparable since kindergarten, which—considering we both just turned thirteen—is basically forever.

When I found out I was going to be winning a Kids' Cartoon Award, I'd asked Anton if he wanted to come watch from the audience.

"Stop. Stop it RIGHT NOW! Are you *serious*?" he'd asked, yanking at his red hair with both of his fists, his freckly pale skin turning pinker by the minute. His blue eyes had gone full saucer on me. "You can actually get me a ticket? To the biggest night of the year?"

Then his cheeks had turned green, and I thought he might throw up from all the excitement.

See, Anton loves all this stuff. He's the biggest *RROS* fan. And not *just* because I play Raj.

In fact, Anton is a walking encyclopedia on everything animation. The desk in his bedroom is covered in cartoon figurines, and his bookshelf is littered with stacks of collectible comic books.

And if it has anything to do with outer space, Anton's your go-to guy.

We make a pretty awesome pair. He's the shortest kid in our class, and I'm, like, a full six inches taller than him, but apart from that, we have almost everything in common.

Anton's also one of the only people who know how nervous I get about stuff like this. Because he's got it way worse. I mean, last year, if a girl in our grade so much as talked to him, sweat would immediately start dripping down the sides of his face.

I guess that's another thing that's different about us. If someone were going to make me blush, it wouldn't be a girl.

It would be a boy.

I hear footsteps running down the hall, and then Anton comes flying into the dressing room followed by his mom, Mrs. Feldman.

"You're officially a Kids' Cartoon Award winner!" he yells before he's even halfway in. We both start screaming in each other's faces and jumping up and down. Drops of green goo fly everywhere.

Mom pleads with me, "Nikhil! Careful!" She's doing all she can to hold on to Streak, but his little body's squirming in her arms, his gray fur sticking out in every direction.

Streak's my other best friend.

When Josh had called to offer me the role of Raj Reddy, he asked Mom if he could get me a gift to celebrate. I'd immediately piped in with, "Can I have a puppy?" I'm pretty sure that's not what Josh had in mind. Even Mom was skeptical. But when the three of us went to the animal shelter and laid eyes on the scrawny puppy cowering in the corner, Mom and I knew immediately that we were taking him home.

"Hey! I have an idea," Josh had said. "How 'bout you name him Streak?"

Mom had shot Josh a questioning look.

"You know, for good luck! 'Cause something tells me Nikhil's going to be on a winning streak here!"

"Josh," Mom had laughed, "that is the cheesiest thing I have ever heard."

But, even though we both made fun of Josh for it, the name just fit. And Streak has been Streak ever since.

Mom's voice is firmer now. "Boys. I'm serious!"

Mrs. Feldman chuckles and squeezes Mom's arm. "Thank you so much for inviting us, Deepa. And Nikhil, we're so proud of you! Anton's going to be talking about this night for the rest of his life!"

I grin at Anton, resisting every urge to pull him into a bear hug so I can cover him in green goo. If he ever had gallons of green sticky stuff poured all over him on stage, I have a feeling he'd pass out.

"Okay, Anton, I'm sorry, but we have to get going!" His mom taps at her wristwatch. "Your dad's already getting the car. And you know we have an early morning tomorrow. We have to drive up north to visit your grandparents."

Anton moans. I'd wanted him to ride home in the limo with us tonight, but Mrs. Feldman had said that "wouldn't work" since they had family "obligations."

We both stick our tongues out at each other and roll our eyes. Then Anton flashes me a Vulcan salute.

I return it.

"You're basically in the superhero hall of fame

now," he says. "Which we all know is the greatest achievement ever." And then he and Mrs. Feldman are gone just as quickly as they came in.

Mom points toward the bathroom, and I make my way past the enormous basket of candy that the network sent. I ignore the temptation to grab a handful of peanut butter cups with my still-green hand.

I'm just about to head through the doorway when I turn back to her and Josh.

I hesitate.

"Hey," I say, not sure I want to hear the answer to my question. "Was I okay out there?" I swallow. "I mean, I had a whole speech planned. I don't know what happened."

Josh's eyebrows rise in surprise. "You were great! You're a star, Nikhil!"

"It was very sweet," Mom agrees.

I close the door and lean up against it.

I feel like I can finally breathe.

CHAPTER 3

I toss my gooey clothes into a pile on the bathroom floor and hop in the shower, letting the hot, steamy water rinse away all the green.

I'm toweling my hair dry in front of the mirror when I hear Mom's voice on the other side of the door.

"You're sure it won't be a problem, right?"

"I think we've got it all figured out," Josh answers.

What won't be a problem? I wonder.

It's hard to hear them, and I'm tempted to turn off the bathroom fan. But from their hushed tones, I have a feeling they don't want me to listen.

I tiptoe to the door and press my ear against it.

"I had to do a little convincing with the network,"

Josh continues. "But we found a great studio out there that we can record him from. It's surprisingly state of the art. Although it wasn't easy, Deepa! Your family lives in the middle of nowhere!"

Mom exhales through her nose. "You're telling me!"

What are they talking about?

There's a moment of silence, and then Josh lowers his voice. "How does Nikhil feel about it?"

I hear footsteps, like someone's pacing.

"I still have to tell him." Mom sighs.

Tell me what?

There's a knock on the bathroom door, and I almost bang my head. Then Mom calls out, "Nikhil, are you finished in there?"

I throw on a pair of jeans and a T-shirt—my *own*, which I brought from home—slide my arms into my hoodie, and open the bathroom door. I scoop up Streak. "What are you guys whispering about out here?"

Josh glances at Mom like a deer caught in head-lights. Then he slowly peels himself up off the couch. "Well, that's my cue! The limo's waiting for the two of you, as planned. Congrats again, Nikhil!" He points at the trophy on the dressing room table. "We're all so proud of you!" Then he shoots me a double thumbs-up and awkwardly closes the door behind him.

"Ready to go?" Mom asks.

But I linger by the bathroom. "What haven't you told me yet?"

"Let's talk in the car, okay?" she says. She starts gathering up our stuff, packing everything into a roller bag.

We sit in silence for a few minutes as our limo winds its way through the Hollywood Hills. Out the window, the lights of the city glitter to the edge of the horizon. When I squint, they morph into a blanket of stars, and I can almost imagine the cartoon version of me soaring across the galaxy.

I turn to face Mom. She's sitting in the row of seats across from me, the suitcase with the basket of candy and my trophy on the floor of the limo between us. Streak rests his head on my lap.

"So?" I ask. "What was all that whispering?"

She runs her hand along the empty car seat.

"Nikhil. I'm sorry for not talking to you about this sooner, but I wanted to make sure we were really going to do this before I . . . well, before I bothered you about it."

"Do what?" Something in the tone of her voice makes me nervous.

She pushes her hair behind her ear. "Well, I spoke to your nani a few weeks ago. She called me from Ohio. I guess your nana isn't doing so great. He's been having some health problems. For a while now."

My family is from the state of Gujarat in India, and Nana and Nani are what I call my grandparents. But it's not like the "nana" a lot of my friends call their grandmothers. It's pronounced "Nah-nah" and "Nah-nee." "Nana" is for your grandfather on your mom's side, and "nani" is for your grandmother.

"Is he going to be okay?" I ask.

A crease forms along her forehead. "I'm not sure. He has a heart condition, which maybe on its own would be more treatable, but his kidneys aren't in good shape either. And, unfortunately, treating the heart is hard on the kidneys, and treating the kidneys is hard on the heart. So, I don't know . . ." Her voice trails off. "Your nani thinks it would be a good idea for us to come home and . . . help."

I feel my stomach clenching. Hearts and kidneys sound pretty serious to me. "Okay."

I don't know my grandparents well, certainly not like Anton knows his.

I was born in Ohio, where they live. But when I was really young, my mom and dad got divorced, and

Mom and I moved to Los Angeles. My dad isn't in the picture anymore, and honestly, neither are Nana and Nani. We video-call them for birthdays or the occasional holiday, but we've only visited them once. And that was years ago.

Ever since I was really little, "family" has just been Mom and me. The two of us taking on the whole world. And then, a few years ago, we added Streak.

"When would we go?" I ask.

"I think soon." She chews on her lower lip. "Nikhil, I'm not sure how you'll feel about this, but . . ." She leans forward. "I'd like to move us there. For a little while. With the school year starting soon, and not knowing how long we'll need to stay, I was thinking you could start the eighth grade there, and then we'll see how things go. I mean, don't get me wrong, it wouldn't be forever. Just for as long as Nani needs our help. Or until Nana . . ."

"Until Nana . . . ? Until Nana what?"

But Mom doesn't answer, which makes me feel even more nervous. How sick *is* he?

I try to process what she's saying. "Wait, but, how can we move? I mean, I already have my school. Here. And how would I record *RROS*?"

"That's what Josh and I were speaking about. He

found a studio near Nana and Nani's house. They can record you remotely."

"Wait. What?" My nerves are turning into panic, and my voice comes out sharper than I expect it to. I know I should be thinking about Nana, but I don't want to leave home. Not for so long. "Why would you talk to Josh about . . . *moving*, before talking to me?"

"Because, Nikhil, I wanted to make sure this was a possibility. I know how important the show is!" Her voice softens. "Listen, this wasn't an easy decision for me either. But I think this is something we *need* to do. Besides"—she keeps going, and now it sounds like she's trying to find a silver lining to this—"you're only young once. You'll never get to be a middle schooler again, you know? It might be nice for you to see the world outside all this"—she gestures to the trophy—"all this Hollywood stuff."

I want to say, *But I love all this Hollywood stuff!* Instead, I say, "What about *your* job?"

"You know I work from home. I can do my job anywhere."

I stare at her. "So, that's it? We're just moving?"

Mom ducks down across the limo and sits next to me. "I know it might feel scary, Nikhil, but—"

"What if I don't *want* to move?"

I think about Anton and how excited we've been to start the eighth grade. How we were finally going to be the kids who the rest of the school looks up to. I think about being at the recording studio every week, and taking Streak to the dog park, and all the things I love about Los Angeles.

I don't want things to change. Just thinking about it makes my stomach hurt.

But it seems like Mom's already made up her mind. And I don't know what else to say that will convince her otherwise.

So instead I say the thing we never talk about, the thing I know I shouldn't. "But you don't even like Nana! You've *never* liked him!"

As soon as it comes out, I wish I could take it back.

Even Streak seems to know it was wrong. He whimpers, lifting his head in my lap.

Mom's quiet for what feels like an eternity.

Then she says, "Maybe that's why I want to go back, Nikhil. Maybe I need to make things right with Nana before . . . before it's too late."

I look up and catch her wiping away a tear.

I don't *want* to leave home.

But it sounds like Nana is really sick. And that

Nani could use our help.

And it's pretty clear that Mom wants to be there.

She reaches down and squeezes my hand, and I squeeze hers back.

Outside the window, the lights of the city go flying by.

It isn't forever, I tell myself. *It isn't forever.*

CHAPTER 4

"IT'S THE LAND OF CORNFIELDS!"

I whisper-shout into my phone, trying not to let Mom hear the groan in my voice. Which isn't easy, considering I'm sitting right behind her in the back of our station wagon.

Five days ago, we piled our suitcases into Mom's Subaru. Then we went through the house one last time, pulling all the curtains shut and locking all the doors. We dropped the keys—and a bunch of Mom's plants—at our neighbor's, who promised to keep an eye on things until we got back.

Then, Mom pulled onto the highway and headed east.

Every day, for seven long hours, Mom drove and drove and drove and drove—through cactus-filled deserts, up curvy mountain roads, and over endless stretches of highways—until we finally stopped each night at a motel. In the morning, we'd grab breakfast and start driving all over again. You wouldn't believe how easy it is to find an IHOP or a Denny's on the way to Ohio. It's a good thing we're almost at Nana and Nani's house, because I'm this close to turning into a pancake.

Mom tried to find ways to keep the trip fun for me.

"This is Captain Mom checking in with Copilot Nikhil. Can I get an update on how many more exits until the nearest gas station?" she'd ask, making her voice sound like it was coming through an intercom. "Copy that, Captain Mom. This is Copilot Nikhil guiding you in for a landing at the next refueling dock," I'd play along, searching for gas stations on the GPS.

But with every passing mile—no matter how hard we scream-sang, totally off-key but with all our hearts, to "This Is Me" from *The Greatest Showman*, or how excited we got when we spotted a license plate from Hawaii—I couldn't shake the feeling that our house was disappearing into a tiny dot behind us.

And at the last rest stop, I finally asked Mom if I could video-call Anton.

Which is why I'm now crouched up against the window in the back seat with Streak curled against my leg in his harness. My headphones are in, so Mom doesn't hear when Anton shouts back, "*WHAT* DID YOU SAY?"

I glance up at her. She's leaned halfway over the steering wheel, squinting to make sure she doesn't miss the turn into her old neighborhood. With one hand, she pushes her long, curly hair out of her face. Then, without taking her eyes off the road, she digs into a crumpled-up takeout bag in the passenger seat. She sticks a stale, cold french fry in her mouth.

I think that fry is from yesterday, but I bet it still tastes good.

I bring my phone closer to my face so Anton can read my lips. "CORNFIELDS! UGH! THEY'RE EVERYWHERE!"

I flip my phone camera toward the window. When I turn it back around, I roll my eyes, but to my surprise Anton's beaming.

"Nikhil, I've been googling all about Ohio!" He whips out a vintage comic book with an illustrated UFO on the cover. He shoves it in front of his iPad.

"See this?" The title comes into focus. It says, *Incredible Sightings of UFOs and the Aliens Who Fly Them.* Then, the book disappears out of frame. "According to this, cornfields make the perfect landing pads for UFOs! And"—his eyes grow wider— "according to the internet, Ohio cornfields have the highest number of crop circle formations in the *entire* country! So, hello? That means UFOs have definitely landed there! Not to mention"—now he stands up and starts pacing around his room—"there's this place called Wright-Patterson Air Force Base—in Ohio!— where the government is hiding ALIENS IN THE BASEMENT!"

"What?" I say. "That can't be true, can it?"

"Yeah. It is! And it's not that far from your grand-parents'!"

I feel a spark of excitement forming in my belly. I'm definitely looking that up later.

Mom slams the brakes, and Streak and I lurch against our seatbelts. "Sorry! I missed the turn! Every-one okay back there?"

"I have to call you later, Anton. I should probably help navigate." I pocket my phone as Mom makes a U-turn. "Back on track, Captain?"

"Mm-hmm." She purses her lips and lets out a

long, steady stream of air. When I catch her reflection in the rearview mirror, her eyebrows are knitted tightly together.

I can tell Mom's nervous today. About seeing Nana and Nani.

Whenever she talks to Nana on the phone, her voice always sounds strained. And her conversations are really short.

Which is exactly how I sound when *my* dad calls.

When I was two years old, my parents got divorced. Pretty soon after, my dad got remarried and moved to Texas. And a few months later, Mom and I moved to Los Angeles.

In the beginning, Dad would come to visit, or he'd fly me out to see him. But then he and his new wife had kids of their own, and our trips became less and less frequent.

Until eventually they stopped.

When he calls me now, we just don't have that much to talk about. So, I always get off the phone pretty quickly.

Mom makes a right turn onto a long cul-de-sac. Tall trees with droopy branches line the sidewalks, and the houses all look similar: redbrick boxes with white- or gray-painted second stories. Black shutters frame the windows, and a couple of American flags dot the neighborhood.

Mom pulls into a driveway about halfway down the street.

We sit inside the car, the doors still locked, for what feels like five whole minutes, until she finally says, "Well. Shall we?"

I nod, letting myself out. The humidity makes my shirt stick to my skin. Our suitcases are still piled in the back, but I grab the duffel bag on the seat beside me. Streak jumps out, and I slip his leash into his collar.

Mom checks her reflection in the driver's-side window. She pulls her hair into a ponytail and blots her lips together, even though she isn't wearing any lipstick.

We walk up to Nana and Nani's porch. Just as Mom's about to ring the doorbell, the front door opens.

It's Nani.

She has the same hair as Mom, but with streaks of gray in it, and her eyes crinkle when she smiles.

"Deepa!" She clasps her hands against her own cheeks. "You're here after so long!"

Mom rubs her elbow. And then she does something I don't remember ever seeing her do.

She lowers her head and bows down to touch Nani's feet with her fingertips. Nani rests her hand on top of Mom's head. "Come, come," Nani says, quickly lifting Mom up. "There's no need for that." When she hugs Mom, I see a wetness in Nani's eyes.

I'm not sure if I should bow down to Nani or not. I know it's a way to show respect to your elders, and that when they place their hand on your head, they're offering their blessings to you. But I've never actually done it before.

I'm not even sure *how* you're supposed to do it.

I start to lower my head, but thankfully Nani stops me, grabbing my cheeks between her fingers and squeezing them. "And here's my little actor!" she laughs. "Or should I say *big* actor? Look how tall you are! My movie star!" She pulls me into her, and I'm enveloped in her flowery purple blouse. I smell a faint hint of soap mixed with Indian spices.

Streak barks, as if he wants a hug, too, and Nani jumps back like three feet. "Oh!" She clutches her hand to her chest. "And this must be your dog!"

Now Streak is spinning in circles at her feet, yipping excitedly.

"Don't be scared," I say. "He's super friendly. Right, Streak?"

I scoop him up and hold his wriggling face close to hers. She reaches out like she wants to pet him, but her fingers are curled back at a safe distance.

Behind Nani, the door opens and Nana slowly steps out onto the porch.

Streak's body tenses in my arms.

Nana rests his hand on Nani's shoulder for support. His fingers tremble against her shirt.

Nana's thin and just a little taller than Nani. It's obvious that he shaved this morning, but there are one or two spots of gray stubble that he must have missed, and his hair is tousled, like maybe he was napping. He wears a lightly wrinkled white kurta that hangs over his brown dress pants, and his feet are slipped loosely inside a pair of chappals.

"Look, Amar, look who's here!" Nani reaches up and grasps his hand. Nana steadies himself against the doorframe.

"Hi, Dad," Mom says softly.

Nana holds her gaze and nods, but he doesn't say anything.

It gets quiet for so long that I wonder if he's waiting for us to bow down to him.

"Come, come!" Nani finally breaks the silence. "Why are we standing in this heat? I made chai. And some snacks." She motions for us to follow her inside. "I'm so glad you two are here!"

Streak barks his approval, and Nani jumps again.

"Oh! I'm sorry," she says. "I mean all *three* of you!"

CHAPTER 5

Nani brings out a seemingly endless parade of food, arranging tray after tray on the coffee table while Mom and I settle into the sofa.

"Homemade khaman!" Nani points at one platter. Then she slides another in front of me. It's piled high with golden-brown fritters, the steam still rising off them. "And some vegetable bhajiyas!" She sets a small steel bowl on the table. "You can dip everything in this chutney! Oh, and I almost forgot the sweets!"

She hurries back into the kitchen.

Nana rests his fingers on the arm of his recliner and starts to lower himself in. He grimaces, making a wheezing noise, and Mom leans forward, reaching a hand out to him. But Nana shakes his head. He sinks into the chair with a heavy sigh.

Mom looks down at her lap. Then she smiles brightly. "This is so much food! She didn't need to make all this. It must have been a lot of work."

Nana grunts, arranging a pillow behind his back. "In our culture, we always feed our guests."

Mom lets out a half laugh that seems to stick in her throat. "Well, we're not *guests*. We're family."

"Family that hasn't visited in a long time. So . . ." Nana trails off.

Nani comes whirling back in with more food. But this time it's sugary sweets. Jalebis: deep-fried, pretzel-shaped dough rings soaked in syrup. They're sticky and amber colored, and their swirly spirals glisten like honey.

I reach for one. So does Streak. He stretches his neck toward the coffee table, his nose twitching back and forth.

"Nice try, Streak. These are not for you!"

"Oh!" Nani wrings her hands. "He must be hungry, too, no?"

"He's *always* hungry!" I laugh. "But we have dog food for him. Which he gets to eat later."

"Well, at least let me get him some water!" She

scurries off to the kitchen once again.

"Do you take care of the dog?" Nana asks, and there's a sternness in his voice. "Walk him? Train him properly? Or do you make your mom do all the work?"

Mom bristles, moving a few inches closer to me on the sofa. "Nikhil is a very responsible boy." She pats my knee. "He takes good care of Streak."

"Hmm," Nana says.

The jalebi is halfway in my mouth when Nana mutters under his breath, "But Nikhil can answer for himself, no?"

I giggle uncomfortably, my mouth full of food.

Nani comes back in and sets down a bowl of water for Streak. Then she sits up tall in the armchair next to the reading lamp. "Deepa, I've made up the guest room for you. It has its own bathroom, so you should be comfortable there. And Nikhil, you can stay in your mom's old room, okay?" Nani's eyes shine. "I got it ready especially for you."

I nod. "Thank you."

"So, Dad," Mom asks. "How have you been feeling? How's your health?"

A flicker of annoyance darts across Nana's face. "I'm fine. You didn't have to run all the way across the country like this. I had some swelling in my legs and some coughing, but the doctor adjusted my medication, and I'm better now. Everybody can stop worrying. I'm not going anywhere."

I feel a sense of relief wash over me. But then, I see how tightly Nani's lips are pressed together.

Mom rubs her hands along the front of her thighs. "Nobody's worried. Nikhil and I just wanted to come spend some time here, that's all." Then she adds, with a little more edge, "You know, after so long."

I take in Nana and Nani's living room. A bookshelf on one end fills half the wall. A small bronze statue of the Lord Ganesh sits on the mantel above the fireplace. And on the table next to Nana's chair rest a few framed photographs.

One is a picture of Mom and Dad at their wedding. My dad is Indian American, too, and he's wearing a dark red turban and kurta. Mom's in a matching sari with a gold border. Shiny jewels dangle from her ears, and a garland of roses hangs from her neck all the way to her knees. She looks like she could be in a magazine.

Except there's a funny expression on her face that makes it hard to tell if she's happy.

Mom must notice the photograph, too, because

she quietly asks, "Dad, why do you have that picture out?"

"Why wouldn't I?" Nana answers. "You might not be married anymore, but he's still my son-in-law." He looks up at Mom, like he's challenging her to defy him.

"Oh, really?" Mom sticks her chin out. "You know he has a whole other family now, right?"

Nani clasps her hands together under her chin. "Okay, okay. Let's not argue. You just got here, and we're all having a good time. It's a nice picture, that's all. Deepa, you look so pretty in it."

Mom rolls her eyes. "Well, I'd be happy to send you another picture where I look pretty, if that's what you're looking for."

Nani walks over to the end table and picks up the frame. "I'll put it away. Okay? Don't be upset. Not now." Then she looks right at Nana and says, "Amar. Enough!"

Nana shakes his head, and I see something flash behind his eyes, but he doesn't say another word.

Nani extends her hand out to me. "Nikhil, beta, come! Let me show you your bedroom, okay?"

I grab my duffel bag from beside the sofa, and

Streak and I follow Nani down the hall to Mom's old room.

The door makes a squeaking noise as it opens over a dark maroon carpet. In the corner, a comforter, patterned with pink, purple, and blue tulips, is draped over a twin bed. Lace curtains flutter in an open window over a small desk. And a cloth mural on the wall is embroidered with Indian village women engaged in a traditional stick dance.

"What do you think?" Nani asks, smiling. "Do you like it?"

"Oh!" I try to hide the disappointment in my voice. "It's *so* nice. Is this, um, how it looked when Mom was a kid?"

"No, no!" Nani laughs. "When your mom was a little girl, she had the whole room set up for a princess! She loved everything princess! Princess table, princess chair, princess furniture. Princess posters."

"What? No way!" Now I'm laughing, too. "That doesn't sound like Mom at all!"

"Well, it was! When she was a little girl, anyway."

Streak jumps up on the bed and curls himself into a little ball.

"You both must be tired, huh? From the drive?"

Nani pats my shoulder. "Should I leave you alone for a while?"

"Okay." I nod.

Nani closes the door behind her, and I hop up onto the bed next to Streak.

He peers up at me with one eye.

I hear the sound of a suitcase being dragged down the hall, and then Nani's voice showing Mom her room.

I guess Mom didn't stay to talk to Nana much longer. Is this what it's going to be like every day here? All that tension between them?

I unzip my duffel bag and unwrap my Kids' Cartoon Award trophy. I lean across the end of the bed and set it on the desk.

CHAPTER 6

"**L**ots of firsts today, huh?" Mom casually sticks the tip of her finger in her mouth. Then, before I have a second to react, she reaches across the car, puts her finger in my ear, and gives me a wet willy. I squirm around in my seatbelt.

"Staaaahp!" I squeal. "Eyes on the road, please!"

It's the first day of school, and I know Mom's trying to keep things upbeat.

This morning, the move hit me all over again.

I should be in Los Angeles today. Starting the eighth grade. With Anton.

I wanted to call him when I woke up, but Mom reminded me that LA is three hours behind Ohio, which means at seven a.m. here, it was only four a.m. his time. He would have been fast asleep.

I feel a dull ache in the pit of my stomach.

I try to picture what he's doing right now. He's probably drooling into his pillow next to that glowing red lava lamp he refuses to ever turn off. I bet he's wearing that threadbare NASA T-shirt he wore to every sleepover we ever had.

A smile creeps across my face.

This afternoon is another first. I get to see the new studio here and record *RROS*.

"I'll pick you up right after school to take you to work, okay, busy boy?" Mom says as we pull up to the row of cars dropping kids off in front of the school. I'm halfway out the door when she reaches for my hand. "Hey, Nikhil? Have fun today, okay?"

I glance over my shoulder. The entire front lawn of the school is buzzing with kids. Kids hovered over each other's phones. Kids racing up the concrete path to the front entrance of the school. Kids throwing their arms around each other's shoulders, laughing.

That ache in my stomach comes back. I force myself to put on a brave face. I grip Mom's hand. Then I quickly unclasp my fingers. It's probably not a good idea to be seen holding your mom's hand on the first day of school. "Love you, Mom."

Sycamore Middle School is bigger than I expected. Large brick buildings sprawl across a grassy lawn. Tall trees rustle in the gentle breeze, and an LED marquee announces, "Welcome Back Sycamore Prairie Dogs!" Every time the words scroll across the marquee, a digital animal that looks like a squirrel twirls around and does backflips.

Is that a prairie dog? What is a *prairie dog*, anyway?

I suddenly feel so alone.

Relax, I tell myself. *You survived having goo poured on you on national TV! How bad can this be?*

I start cutting across the lawn when I realize that I have no idea where I'm even going. I see another kid, with a pair of earbuds in, leaving a group of friends, and I decide to take a chance. I tap him on the shoulder. He casts a glance my way and then slides the earbuds out of his ears. I hear the tinny sounds of a pop song still playing.

"Hey," I say, and he must see the anxiety on my face, because he asks, "New here?"

"Is it that obvious?" I bite my lip.

"Um. Maybe?" He chuckles. Two dimples form along his dark brown cheeks. He's Black, just a little taller than me, and is sporting a short afro.

"I'm DeSean." He waves even though we're standing right in front of each other.

"I'm Nikhil." I wave back, and for some reason it makes both of us laugh.

"Wait a minute!" He snaps his fingers, his hazel eyes sparkling in the sun. "I think I've seen you before!"

The muscles in my face tighten. I'm not ready for anyone to recognize me just yet.

The thing about playing a cartoon character is that for the most part, people can't really place you. Even if you've watched every episode of *RROS*, you're still seeing an animated drawing, not me. So, unless you saw my picture in a magazine, or watched the Kids' Cartoon Awards, or saw one of the few videos I've made for social media, you wouldn't meet me and think, *Hey, you must be Raj Reddy!*

When someone does recognize me, it can be a lot of pressure. Kids will ask me to "do the voice," or take a picture with them, or record a video of me on their phone.

I steel myself, waiting for DeSean to put it together.

But instead, he points at me. "I think you live in

my neighborhood! Do you have, like, a dog that you walk sometimes?"

I breathe a sigh of relief. "Yes! My dog, Streak! Wait, you live on Sommers Avenue?"

"Uh-huh! Since I was a baby!" he says, and he uses this old-timey voice that makes me laugh again.

DeSean hikes up his burnt orange backpack, and I notice he has an Ohio State football pin on the strap. There's a Black Lives Matter pin just below it and a few hand-drawn music notes in all different colors of faded Sharpie.

He stuffs his earbuds into the front pocket of his jeans. "So, want some help figuring out where to go?"

"That would be amazing!"

We fall in step with each other and wait our turn in line at a folding table outside the main office to get our locker assignments. When we get to the front, a white teacher with red cat-eye glasses perched on top of her head and a name tag that reads, *Bring on the drama! I'm Mrs. Reed!* practically leaps out of her chair. Her dark brown hair catches the light as she stretches her arms our way and grabs at the air in front of her. "There you are! I've been waiting for you!" she singsongs. "How's my little superstar?"

I feel that panic rising again. *Does Mrs. Reed know who I am?*

But then, she clutches DeSean's shoulders. "You and I need to have a talk about the school musical! And soon!" She motions at the kid behind us to move up to the other teacher checking people in. Then she drops her voice to a faux whisper. "This is going to be *your* year!" She lowers her glasses over her eyes. It magnifies her teal eye shadow. A tiny set of comedy and tragedy masks dangles from the gold chain attached to the temple of her glasses.

She looks intently at DeSean. "I am determined to showcase your talent before I lose you forever"—she blanches—"to the high school!"

DeSean grins. "Thanks, Mrs. Reed. I'm super excited about it! I've been working on a ton of music over the summer!"

"And who do we have here?" She glances at me over the rim of her glasses.

"Oh. Hi. I'm Nikhil," I say. "Nikhil Shah."

"Shah, Shah, Shah." She flips through pages of printed-out names in a binder. "Here you are. You're new, I see. Welcome!" She scrawls my locker number and combination on a slip of paper and hands it to me. "Now, in case it isn't obvious"—she flutters her hand just below the comedy and tragedy masks hanging from her glasses—"I'm the drama teacher here. I'm sure DeSean will tell you all about it, but we put on a great musical every year! Everyone's encouraged to audition! Do you have any interest in the dramatic arts, Nikhil?"

"Oh. Well, actually . . ." I hesitate.

Before I can come up with an answer, she jumps back in. "Cat got your tongue? Trust me, if you come audition for the musical, I'll help you find that little voice! I have a feeling it's tucked away *somewhere* inside there."

The rest of the morning goes by quickly. To my relief, in the first three periods, no one seems to know who I am. I guess it helps that eighth graders don't generally greet you with "So, what do you do for a living?"

With each passing class, I keep one eye on the clock, waiting until the end of the day, when I can finally get into the recording studio.

This week's episode of *RROS* is all about this alien on the planet Xacronium-11. He's a troublemaker, always using his three antennae to get up to no good. But when Raj enlists him to help save the galaxy, he comes into his own, and they totally hit it off.

I run into DeSean in the hallway before last period. It turns out we're both in the same math class. We file in and grab seats right next to each other. An Asian girl with bangs and short hair held back by two large clips bounds in and elbow-bumps DeSean. She's wearing a denim jacket over zippered cargo pants and a pair of camouflage high-tops. DeSean hops out of his chair to hug her.

When she smiles big at me, I find myself grinning back before she even says, "Hiya! I'm Monica! Kim. Monica Kim!"

"Nikhil. Shah." I nod.

A flicker of—I'm not sure what—passes across Monica's face.

The teacher walks in and starts writing *Mrs. Gonzalez, 8th Grade Math* on the whiteboard as Monica slides into the desk next to mine.

She purses her lips to one side. Her eyes linger on me.

"What?" I whisper.

"Nothing." She slides her phone out of her book bag and hides it under her notebook. I feel an uneasy knot forming somewhere deep inside my belly.

"This year we're going to be covering a lot of fun topics!" Mrs. Gonzalez is scrawling on the whiteboard.

"Like *repeating* decimals! And *irrational* numbers!" She laughs to herself. "And no, that doesn't mean they make bad decisions!"

Monica turns her phone toward me. "Is this you?" she whispers.

On her screen are a bunch of YouTube videos. They're all of me, standing at the podium at the Kids' Cartoon Awards, right before the goo dropped.

"Oh, um. No. I mean, not really," I mutter.

"Are you sure?" She hits Play on one of them, and she must not realize how loud her volume's turned up, because it suddenly blares, "I'm Raj Reddy!" The video must be on a loop, because it keeps saying the same line. Over and over again.

"I'm Raj Reddy! I'm Raj Reddy!"

DeSean raises his eyebrows. "Wait! Is that *you*? No way! I love that show!"

"Monica! What's going on over there? No phones in the classroom!" Mrs. Gonzalez tries to reprimand her, but a group of students are now clustered around Monica's desk. One of them grabs her phone and starts passing it around.

"I'm so sorry!" Monica mouths my way, trying to get her phone back.

A kid raises his hand for a high five. "Awesome!"

he says. "Wanna hang at my house after school?"

"Oh, well, actually . . ."

"Wait, hold on! Smiiiiile." He whips his phone out, and suddenly he's crouching down next to my desk, taking a selfie with me. Another kid makes a megaphone with her hands and calls out, "Are you ready, Reddy?"

"Class! Please! Settle down!" Mrs. Gonzalez is almost yelling now.

A group of kids start chanting, "Do the voice! Do the voice! Do the voice!"

I turn to DeSean. He flips his palms up and shrugs.

"Okay, okay, okay." I run my fingers along the back of my neck to try to let some air inside my shirt. My cheeks are so hot they feel like they're on fire.

I stand up, and the room grows quiet. Even Mrs. Gonzalez seems to be waiting.

"Um. Okay," I say. "Here goes." Then, I grin as wide as I can and pitch my voice up ever so slightly. "I'm Raj Reddy!"

The whole class erupts, "WOOOOOOOT!"

CHAPTER 7

"**O**kay, he can only sign one more autograph!" DeSean announces. A collective groan goes up from the few remaining kids huddled around my locker. "Sorry, people! We've got places to be! Our moms are waiting for us in the carpool line!" He points at the curly-haired boy standing in front of me. "You're the last one!"

Somebody mutters, "Aw, really? I waited forever!" and I hear someone else say, "This always happens to me! I'm so unlucky!" as they shuffle down the hallway.

"I can sign more tomorrow!" I yell. I turn to the curly-haired kid looking up at me. He seems young.

Like a sixth grader.

"Do you have a piece of paper or something?" I ask. "That you want me to sign?"

His eyes grow into dinner plates. "No. No, I don't."

DeSean reaches into his backpack and tears a page out of his notebook. "Want to use this?"

"Wait," the kid says. He slides an iPhone out of his pocket, flips it over so its silvery back faces up, and holds it to me like an offering. "Just sign this."

"Ooooh." I pull the Sharpie that Mrs. Gonzalez had loaned me after class into my chest. "I . . . um, I *really* don't think that's a good idea." I pat my pockets, searching for another pen. "I mean, this marker is permanent."

"I know," the kid says, and his lower lip quivers. "I want to keep your signature forever."

I make a helpless face at DeSean. He shrugs back at me.

"Um . . . okay?" I turn to the kid. "I mean, if you insist."

As soon as I finish, DeSean claps me on the back. "Let's get out of here!"

We're halfway down the hall when I hear footsteps racing up behind us. "Nikhil! DeSean! Wait up!"

It's Monica. With another kid right behind her.

"I'm so sorry about what happened in class!" She catches her breath as she approaches us. "It's just . . ." She pushes her hair behind her ears. "I'm a really big *RROS* fan. I watch it all the time."

"Thanks," I say, and there's something about how sincerely she says it that feels different from the explosion of attention I just got.

"I mean, it's such a good show, but also"—she swallows, and a hint of embarrassment passes over her face—"well, I think it's cool that you're Asian!" She shakes her head. "That's not what I meant! Sorry!" Now she looks full-on mortified. "I mean, I'm Korean, so . . ." She holds her hands up. "What I'm trying to say is . . ." She pauses. "I just think it's cool you're Asian, and you're the lead. That's all." She peers up at me. "Is that weird?"

I let out a small chuckle. "I don't think that's weird." I eye the kid behind her, but he's just staring at the floor. "It's actually really nice."

She exhales. "Also, I saw that interview you did. The one in *Teen Vogue*? And I thought it was really great that you talked about what it's like getting to play an Indian character in it."

"Oh, thanks." I nod.

"You were in *Teen Vogue*?" DeSean's face lights up. "Wow! Nice!"

I feel some of Monica's embarrassment creeping up on me, but before I have to respond, she says, "Wait. Why are you *here*? At Sycamore? Don't you live in Los Angeles?"

"Oh, um . . ." I hesitate. "Well, we just moved here 'cause . . ." Now I'm the one who's looking at the floor. "My grandfather's kinda sick. So, my mom and I are here to . . . help out."

DeSean casts a sympathetic look my way. "I'm sorry. I hope he gets better."

Monica and the kid behind her both echo him. "Sorry." And then, Monica throws her hands up in the air. "Oh my gosh! Where are my manners?" She guides the kid into our circle. "This is Mateo!" She does this strange finger wriggle at him, holding her hand out in front of her chin. He does the same back to her, their fingertips grazing each other.

"Mon and I are sort of inseparable." He shrugs.

Mateo's shorter than me, with light brown skin and messy, dark hair that hangs in big curls over his eyes. His backpack is loosely slung off one shoulder, and he's got a sketchbook shoved under his arm. It has a sticker on it that says, *Skateboarding Is Life*.

"Hi." I nod.

He shoves his hair up out of his eyes, and when he looks at me, his smile is all goofy. "Hey," he says. Only, he adds a question mark to the end of it, which makes him sound like a surfer.

Something flips inside my stomach.

My cheeks get warm. And they turn full red when he adds, "I love *RROS*, too." He grins, kind of shyly. "I've been to LA. My tío lives there. Near Venice Beach."

DeSean jiggles his leg. "Guys, I'm sorry, but I gotta run! I have a voice lesson. Wanna sit together at lunch tomorrow?"

"Voice lesson?" I say. "That's cool!" Then I clap my palm to my forehead. "Oh shoot, I have to go, too!"

I almost forgot I have to be at the recording studio today.

DeSean and I take off down the hallway, but just before we turn the corner, I peek back over my shoulder.

Mateo's walking toward the lockers. With Monica.

My stomach flips again.

CHAPTER 8

By the time I get to the parking lot, Mom's leaning across the passenger seat and beckoning at me through the open car window. "Nikhil! Where have you been? We're supposed to be at the recording studio in ten minutes!"

"Sorry!" I hop in, dropping my book bag at my feet. I pull the seatbelt over my shoulder. "I was just talking to some kids."

"Oh yeah?" She pulls out of the carpool line. "Well, that makes me happy! New friends? And on the very first day? I want to hear all about them." She reaches over to ruffle my hair.

I duck away, but I'm smiling.

Mom hits Start on the GPS, and it begins directing us to a place called Big Bob's Audio House.

"How about you, Mom? How was your day?"

"Oh, let me tell you, not exactly a picnic!" she says, making a turn at the light. "I got my desk and all my computer equipment set up in Nana and Nani's basement, but then I spent half the morning on the phone with the cable company trying to get faster internet! You wouldn't believe how long they put me on hold! By the time I actually sat down to work, I had a million emails and phone calls to return. There's just never enough time!"

Mom's got a cool job. She's a graphic designer. Which means she creates logos and websites for companies, designs layouts for magazines, and she's even illustrated book covers. I'm pretty sure I get my artistic side from her.

She used to go into an office every day, but during the pandemic, she set up a home workspace with three large computer screens on her desk. It looked like command central for a spaceship.

Working from home made Mom realize she didn't want to go back to an office full-time, so she left her job and started her own company. In the beginning, she was worried about finding new clients. But after just a couple of months, she was busier than ever.

Plus, she seems a lot happier than she did at her old job.

The GPS announces that we're about to arrive at our destination. Except we're in a residential neighborhood filled with houses that look just like Nana and Nani's.

"This can't be right," I say.

In Los Angeles, the recording studio is behind a pair of tall gates, with a security booth in front. Inside, statues of famous cartoon characters, like Bugs Bunny and Elmer Fudd, line the sidewalk around a glass building with the word "ANIMATION" written across it. It feels like you're at a theme park.

Mom pulls into a driveway, and we both stare up at what looks like, well, a house. Because . . . it *is* a house.

"This is strange," Mom says, scrolling through her emails. "I'm positive this is the address Josh gave me."

"Should we call him?" I ask.

The front door opens, and a white man in jeans and a flannel shirt, who's so tall that he has to duck down to get past the doorframe, steps onto the porch.

"Are you Nikhil?" he calls out, waving at our car. "Don't be shy! I'm Big Bob!"

Mom raises her eyebrows at me over her phone. "Well, I guess this *is* it."

Big Bob walks us through his living room and past a kitchen with linoleum floor tiles. A large gray cat darts past my feet in the hallway. And then we're standing in front of a door with a tin sign nailed to it that reads, *Quiet Please. Recording in Progress.*

Bob opens the door, flips on a light, and the three of us head down a set of stairs.

"Whoa," I whisper. "What is all this stuff?"

Big Bob's entire basement is filled with radios.

They're arranged on tables and shelves, and some of them are so large, they just sit on the floor. There are so many of them that it feels like we're in a museum.

There's a wooden one with ivory buttons that's almost as tall as me and looks like a jukebox. Another one folds into a briefcase, with a hidden compartment that has a pair of headphones stashed inside it. It looks like it could be in a spy movie. I bet Anton would love it.

There's even one of those old-school boom boxes.

The kind Snoopy dances to in reruns of *Peanuts* cartoons.

Bob runs his hand over a small, dark wooden one. "Any idea what this beauty's called?"

I look up at Mom and shrug.

"Don't ask me," Mom says. "That has to be from way before my time."

Bob chuckles, and his smile makes the red-and-white stubble of his beard fan out across his face. "It's from way before *all* our times! This here is a Crosley Harko radio, built in 1921 by a Mr. Powel Crosley Jr." His eyes twinkle. "He built it right around the corner from here, in Cincinnati, Ohio!" He invites me to take a closer look. "He mass-produced these, which meant that for the first time ever, the average person was able to afford a radio. This little machine right here brought the sound of the human voice into regular people's homes for the very first time."

"Wow." I lean in and peer at the brass knobs. "Why do you have all these?"

"Oh, I'm fascinated by this stuff." Bob smiles. "Always have been. So, when I finally quit my day job, I drove around to old antique stores and scoured the internet, and started putting this collection together. And then I bought a bunch of equipment and built out my own recording studio, too. I guess you could say being in the recording business is kind of a dream come true for me, you know?"

Mom puts her arm around me, and I have a feeling it's because she knows that being in the business is a dream come true for me, too.

When I was five years old, she likes to tell me, I'd park myself in front of the TV, and she'd have to pry me away from watching all my favorite cartoons. I'd just sit there for hours, with my jaw hanging open.

When I was ten, I saw the open-call announcement for *Raj Reddy in Outer Space*. There was an ad on TV, sandwiched between two Saturday-morning cartoons, telling kids where to send in audition tapes. I grabbed the remote and turned the volume up. "Mom! Look! They're making a new cartoon, and they want an Indian actor! The character's name is Raj!" She'd come running into the room, and I'd clutched her hand. "Can I audition?"

I'd only seen a few cartoons that had Indian characters in them. Some of them were cool, for sure, but some were offensive. When I'd watch them, I'd feel embarrassed. Like, the character would be so over-the-top, it seemed to be making fun of our culture, or they'd have an accent so thick that it felt like a joke.

And regardless, there just weren't that many Indian characters, period. But Raj was the lead role, and it didn't seem like he was going to be a stereotype.

RROS had done a nationwide search. At first, Mom just recorded me on her phone saying my name and what I loved about cartoons. I did a few impersonations of some of my favorite characters, and then she uploaded the file to a link on the *RROS* website.

Then, we waited.

And waited.

And waited.

For months.

And just when I was pretty sure we were never going to hear anything, Mom got an email asking if she could bring me to the studio for a callback!

Callbacks went on for weeks. But what I remember most is the first time I stepped up to the microphone and put the headphones on. It felt like the whole world was disappearing. Then, Josh had asked me if I could pitch my voice up a little.

I remember saying, "I'm Raj Reddy!" and looking through the glass window of the sound booth and seeing the smiles on the faces of all the producers who were auditioning me.

It felt like magic.

Josh's voice crackles through a set of speakers hanging on Bob's basement wall, snapping me back to reality. "This is Josh Green dialing in from Los Angeles. Are you all set up over there?"

Bob glides over to a desk in the corner of the room and leans over a microphone. "We sure are!" Then he turns to me, rubbing his hands together. "Let's get you in front of the mic!"

Bob guides me into the sound booth right behind his desk and turns on the iPad resting on a music stand. A microphone hangs down over it. He swipes through a few screens until my script pops up. He adjusts the height of the microphone until it's dangling just a few inches away from my mouth. Then he shuts the soundproof door behind him.

And finally, it's just me. All alone in the booth.

The padding that lines the walls makes the room pin-drop quiet. The air hangs completely still.

I lower the headphones over my ears, and it feels like I'm in a secret world that's all my own.

A glass window separates me from where Bob sits at the soundboard. He carefully adjusts the sliders that balance out the audio levels.

Josh's voice comes streaming into my headphones.

"Hey! How are you, buddy? Excited for our first remote session?"

"Uh-huh," I say.

"Great! Let's start at the top. I'll read Commander Marks's lines, and we'll run through the first scene."

I scroll past the title page to the first line of the script.

INT. RAJ REDDY'S BEDROOM - MIDDLE OF THE
NIGHT.
It's quiet. A voice sputters through the watch
on Raj's wrist.

COMMANDER REGINA MARKS
Yo! Are you there, Raj?

Silence from Raj. Maybe even a snore.

COMMANDER REGINA MARKS
Helloooo! Earth to Raj!
Or should I say, Raj *on* Earth! Wake up,
sleepyhead!

Raj shoots straight up in bed, frantically

untangling himself from his sheets. He looks
at his alarm clock and hisses into his watch.

                    RAJ REDDY
    It's three in the morning! Why do you
    always wake me up so early?

                COMMANDER REGINA MARKS
    Because, Raj, you look so *adorable* with
    bedhead!

Raj tries to fix his hair.

                COMMANDER REGINA MARKS
    Raj, you're needed on the planet
    Xacronium-11. Right away! I'll give you
    your instructions on the way there. But
    before you go, I have one question for
    you. Are you ready, Reddy?

Raj is now fully dressed with his jetpack on.

    RAJ REDDY
    Oh, I'm ready, Commander. *I'm Raj Reddy.*

By the time six p.m. rolls around, I've flown to a made-up planet 550 million miles away, become besties with an alien with three unruly antennae, and—once it's all edited together—I'll have saved the entire galaxy in just twenty-two minutes and three commercial breaks.

Josh is thrilled, practically screaming into my headset. "This episode is going to be lit! Nice work, Nikhil!" Bob's face glows when he opens the door to let me out of the booth. And Mom's biting her lower lip, raising the roof with her arms. "You were so funny, Nikhil!"

I scrunch up my face and shake my head at her dancing, but then I join right in.

If Mom was frustrated with her workday before, it sure doesn't seem like it now.

Because of me.

I can't help smiling when she pulls me in for a hug.

CHAPTER 9

B y the time we get to Nana and Nani's, I'm so hungry that my stomach is growling. I open the front door, and the smell of Nani's cooking makes my mouth water.

"You're home!" Nani waltzes out of the kitchen. Streak is right on her heels. He barks his head off and barrels straight for me. Nani raises a finger to her mouth. "Shh! Nana's napping!" But when Streak starts dancing on his back legs and pawing at the air, she claps her hands together and laughs.

I guess Streak is growing on Nani.

"Come, come! You must be hungry!" Nani beckons

to me. "How was your . . . what did you call it? Your recording session?"

There's a fumbling noise in the hallway, and the sound of a door closing.

"Amar, are you awake?" Nani calls out sweetly. Then, more firmly, she says, "It's time for dinner."

Nana's feet shuffle along the floor as he makes his way into the living room, and every few steps, he rests his hand on a piece of furniture to keep his balance.

Mom hovers behind him. She looks at Nani, a question mark in her eyes. Nani motions toward Nana's walking stick, which is leaned up against the wall. Mom picks it up and offers it to him.

"I don't need that," he grumbles, pushing it away. "I can walk by myself."

He makes his way to the head of the dining table, grabs both sides of the back of his chair, and slowly drags it out.

Then he lowers himself into his seat, and we all take our places.

I quietly load up my plate with mung beans and pooris. My mouth is full of food when Nana clears his throat. "Have you finished your homework, Nikhil?"

"We just got home," Mom answers. "He had to

record on his cartoon today. But I'm sure he'll do it right after dinner."

Nana blows on a spoonful of steaming dal. He eyes me over his bowl.

"We, um—" I swallow my food. "We don't have that much, anyway. It's only the first day of school. But, like Mom said, I had to record."

Nana slurps the dal off his spoon. "Homework should always come first," he pronounces. "You should focus on your studies. That's the most important thing!"

"He'll get to it after we eat." Mom takes the lid off a pot of potatoes and ladles some onto her plate. "But his cartoon is important, too, you know!"

I think about how Nana said I should speak for myself. I want to say something more. But I'm not sure what it would be.

"Cartoons won't last forever," Nana says. "But an education will."

Mom exhales through her nose. "Well, Nikhil learns from his cartoon, too. Besides, this could be his full-time career one day. So"—she raises a shoulder—"it's part of his education."

"Cartoons?" Nana's voice is filled with disbelief. "For a career?"

I see a muscle ripple along Mom's jaw.

Nani pats my arm, and I realize my hand is balled into a fist around my napkin. "I've watched some episodes!" she says. "I don't always understand everything. It goes by so fast! And all those planets! They have so many names!" She makes "planet" sound like it's as foreign a word as it is a place. "But I like hearing your voice. I'm so proud of our movie star."

"Thanks, Nani." I look at Nana. I wonder if he likes hearing my voice, too.

"I'm just saying that cartoons are fine for now, but you need to think of his future." Nana looks pointedly at Mom. "You should make sure his other studies don't suffer."

"I think about his future!" Mom's voice is firm. "But who says cartoons can't be a part of that future? Nikhil loves being in the sound booth!" She smiles at me. "Right?"

I nod. I want to say yes, but it feels like my voice is stuck inside my throat now.

"Well, let him do whatever he wants then," Nana grumbles.

Mom knits her brow. "What's that supposed to mean?"

"It means that I am just trying to help my own grandson, but I can't even say anything in my own house!"

Mom makes an exasperated "hah," and Nana digs into his pant pockets and sets a clear, rectangular pill container on the table with a thud.

Each compartment of the pillbox is marked with the first letter of the day of the week. Seven little compartments filled with pills: round pills, oval pills, pills in all different colors.

He flips one of the tops open and shakes the contents into his hand. He claps his palm against his mouth, tilts his head back, and swallows. He reaches for his water. But as soon as he takes a sip, he starts coughing.

A lot.

His whole face turns red, and he presses his fist against his chest, pounding it.

I shoot up out of my chair, my heart racing.

Mom runs behind him and thumps him forcefully on the back. Nani's right on her heels.

Then, just as quickly as his coughing fit started, it ends. Nana rises, gripping the table. "I'm fine!" He waves Mom and Nani off. "I'm fine! Even if nobody in this house will listen to me anymore, I'm fine!"

Mom and Nani are frozen, their upturned palms hanging in the air, as he hobbles toward his bedroom.

"Dad, we do listen to you," Mom says quietly. "We just—"

Nani takes her arm. "Let it go, Deepa. No need to raise anyone's blood pressure." Then she turns to me. "Are you all right, Nikhil?"

"Mm-hmm." I nod.

"Good." Nani forces a smile. She picks up Nana's plate, some food still left on it, and heads into the kitchen. Then she turns back to me and says, "Can I get you some dessert? Maybe some gulab jamun?"

I shake my head. I mumble, "I should probably get to that homework anyhow."

I stack my dinner plate next to where Nani is washing everything at the sink. Mom gently pulls me into the living room and kneels down in front of me. "Hey. You okay?" she asks.

"Mm-hmm."

"Don't let Nana upset you, all right? I'm sorry about that."

I nod.

"Do you want to talk about it?"

I shrug. "I'm okay, Mom."

She eyes me, her forehead wrinkling a little. Then she squeezes my arm. "Well, if you need me, I'm right out here. I'm just going to help Nani with the dishes."

I nod one last time, and Mom kisses me on the cheek.

I head into my room. I dig through my book bag as Streak sniffs his bed. He circles around inside it before flopping down into a little ball.

I sit at the desk and flip open my laptop.

I stare at the computer screen, but it's impossible to focus on my homework.

Did Nani say that *she's* watched *RROS* or that *they've* watched it? Has Nana ever even seen my show? Does he have any idea what I do?

My mind drifts to his pillbox.

I shut my laptop and blow a raspberry.

Why couldn't today have ended at the recording studio?

CHAPTER 10

I avoid having to sign any autographs the next day at school. I guess now that everyone knows I'm sticking around for a while, they figure there's no rush.

In any case, it's nice not feeling like there's a giant spotlight shining on me.

I grab my lunch from my locker and am about to head to the cafeteria when I hear a singsongy voice calling my name.

"Nik-hee-uuul! Nik-heeeeel Sha-uuuh!"

I close my locker to find Mrs. Reed sort of, well, sashaying down the hallway in my direction. She has a black beret on her head and a sparkling purple feather boa wrapped around her neck.

"Somebody failed to mention that they were a professional actor when we met yesterday!" She peers down at me over her glasses. "And here I was babbling on about being the drama teacher and how great the school musical is, and I had no idea I was talking to the star of a television series!"

"Oh, um." I shrug. "Sorry? I . . . probably should have told you."

"Oh, you're sweet!" She waves off my apology. "Listen, I for one appreciate your modesty. It's very refreshing. Especially since most actors seem to be so self-absorbed these days! It's like, do we really need to see every single second of your life on social media? Does anyone care what you ate for lunch?" She throws her arms up in despair. "Or how many beaches you've vacationed on?"

I crumple the top of my lunch bag. "Uh-huh."

"Look, I know you've met DeSean, so I'm sure he'll fill you in on all the details, but"—she twirls the end of her boa in my direction—"you have to come audition for the school musical, okay?"

"Oh. Well." I swallow. I feel a familiar, uncomfortable tingling in my fingers, just thinking about having to be up on stage. In front of people. Staring at me. "I'm not really a singer."

"Well, who is in the eighth grade? Besides, you can act! You're a TV star! The other students would learn so much from you!" She leans in. "Also, I have to tell you. I know *RROS* is for kids, but my husband and I have watched every single episode!" She lets out a giggle. "We even named our cat Commander Marks! Can you believe it?"

"You did?" I try to keep my eyes from looking too surprised. "That's . . . wow, that's really nice of you."

"Eh. To be honest, it was a no-brainer. They have very similar personalities."

"Right. Well, I'll be sure to ask DeSean about the musical. I'm actually going to look for him in the cafeteria right now."

"Great! It'll be such a blast this year, Nikhil. And don't worry about the singing. We do things a little different here at Sycamore. We have auditions early on and then there are just a few light rehearsals in the fall. We don't really get going until after winter break. That way, everyone has plenty of time with the music and the dancing and all of it! By the time spring rolls around, all my little storytellers are ready to take that stage by storm!"

"Nice," I say, trying to back up a little. "Well, I'll talk to DeSean about it for sure."

She smiles. "This year, we're doing a revue of all the great Broadway shows that kids just adore. We'll be singing songs from *Dear Evan Hansen*, *Frozen*, *Matilda*, whatever else I can nab the rights to! We'll do some funny scenes and skits! And to tie it all together, *I'll*"—she lays her hand on her heart—"be writing several original songs and monologues for a Narrator character." She flutters her eyelids. "I happen to be a halfway decent composer, if I do say so myself! Anyhoo, our Narrator is the lead of the show. They'll be our guide on our little tour of Broadway!" She pauses. Then she narrows her eyes at me. "And I just thought of the perfect way to get everyone at this school excited about the musical for once." She winks. "All righty, then. I'll see you at the auditions!"

When I get to the cafeteria, I look over the heads of all the kids, hoping to find DeSean. I breathe a sigh of relief when I see him at a table in the corner. He's sitting across from Monica and—I try to keep my cheeks from twisting into a smile—Mateo.

A couple of girls giggle as I walk by them, and I'm pretty sure a kid in a striped T-shirt sneaks a picture of me on his phone. I dart past them, keeping my head down.

"We saved you a seat!" Monica points at the empty chair across from her. She's wearing a bright purple button-down sweater over a pale shirt with an oversized bow on the front.

"Cool sweater," I say, sliding in across from Mateo.

She covers her mouth in mock surprise. "You like? Jennie wore one just like it to Paris Fashion Week."

"Jennie?" I ask.

"From Blackpink!" She smirks. "Do you know them?"

When I shake my head, she says, "They're, like, one of the best K-pop bands ever! My cousins in Chicago took me to one of their concerts. It was the best night of my life."

Mateo looks up and nods. "Their music is sick."

His sketchbook is flipped open, and I try to peek at what he's drawing, but when he hunches back over the table, his hair blocks everything. A half-eaten slice of pizza and a juice box with a straw sticking out of it are right next to him.

"Cool. I'll have to check them out," I say.

"Did you have trouble finding the cafeteria?" DeSean asks, taking a bite of his sandwich.

His sandwich looks like it could be photographed for a magazine. Curly lettuce leaves stick out between

layers of meats and cheese, and there's a row of vege-
tables on top that look like they've been roasted. The
bread has grill marks on it, and there's even a fancy
toothpick stuck in it.

I set my own lunch bag on the table, trying not
to stare at his food. "Um. Mrs. Reed stopped me on
the way over. She was telling me about the musical? I
guess it's a revue? Whatever that means?"

"Mm," DeSean says, his mouth full. He swallows.
"It just means we're singing a bunch of Broadway
songs and doing skits and stuff!"

"And of course"—Monica flips her hair over her
shoulder—"DeSean's going to be the lead! He would
have been last year, except it always goes to an eighth
grader."

DeSean half rolls his eyes. But there's a smile in
his voice when he says, "We'll see."

"I'm sorry," I say, still staring at his food. "That's
like the nicest sandwich I've ever seen! My mom
never puts toothpicks in my lunch!"

He laughs, shaking his head. "My moms own a
catering company." He slides the untouched half my
way. "They can go a little overboard sometimes. Want
some?"

I'm pretty sure DeSean said "moms," but no one

else seems to react, so I don't either.

"I'm a vegetarian," I say. "But if I weren't . . ."

"My dad's on a plant-based kick!" Monica points at her Tupperware. It's filled with long, see-through noodles. "He says it's better for the environment." Then she smiles. "I'm not mad about it though, 'cause he makes a mean tofu japchae."

I peer inside my bag at the container that Nani packed for me. It's filled with all my favorite leftovers from last night. Right before I got in the car this morning, I'd almost asked Mom for a PB&J sandwich. I'd just never taken Gujarati food to school before.

But it seems like at Sycamore, you can just eat whatever you want.

I'm about to pull the container out when a kid at the table next to us saunters over. He's white with floppy blond hair, and he extends his hand out in front of my face. "Hey, you're the Raj Reddy guy, right?"

"Mm-hmm." I nod, shaking his hand.

"Niiiiice!" He squeezes down tight. "I'm Kyle. I'm on newspaper this year." He squeezes even harder. "Could I, like, maybe interview you sometime? About the cartoon and stuff?"

"Uh-huh, sure," I say. Everyone at our table leans in a little.

"Really?" His eyes light up.

"Yeah."

"Suh-weet!" He lets go of my hand and spins around. He double high-fives the kid still sitting at his table. Then he turns back to me. Very slowly. "Um . . . I actually haven't asked our newspaper teacher about this yet. Or come up with any questions. Or, thought about *when* to do the interview." His eyebrows slide together. "Soooo . . . can I get back to you about all that?"

"Of course," I say. I hear Monica, Mateo, and DeSean suppressing giggles.

As soon as Kyle sits back down, DeSean whispers, "Oh, man. Is it hard dealing with that?"

"I mean, that doesn't really happen to me all the time," I say.

Monica presses a finger against her lips. "But didn't the kids at your old school ask you for interviews and stuff?"

"A little. But I've known a lot of them since kindergarten. So it just wasn't a big deal!" I answer.

The truth is, the kids at my old school got really excited about me for a while, but then Anton and I just sort of slipped into the background again. Like, normal. "I mean, I have to do interviews sometimes.

Like"—I gesture at Monica—"that *Teen Vogue* one."

DeSean cups his fingers against his temples, and then his hands explode like fireworks. "I can't even imagine getting interviewed like that! *Teen Vogue!*"

"Well, you better start!" Monica says. Then she announces, "DeSean's going to be on Broadway one day. Mark my words!"

"He's a total star," Mateo says. Then he leans over and slurps on the straw sticking out of his juice box.

How does someone make slurping on boxed juice seem . . . I don't know, *nice*?

DeSean shakes his head. "Whatever," he laughs, even though his dimples are popping out. Then he pivots around to face me. "Speaking of Broadway, do you think you'll audition for the musical?" He tugs on the sleeve of his rugby shirt. "I don't know what Mrs. Reed told you, but it's a lot of fun! And auditions are really easy! You just show up, and she teaches us a song right there on the spot."

"Well, of course you're auditioning!" Monica says incredulously. "You must have been in all the shows at your old school! Right?"

"Um." I bite my lip. "Not really. I mean, we didn't even have a musical! We didn't even have an arts program!" Mateo looks up from his sketchbook in disbelief. "It's true!" I say. "But even if we did—" I catch myself.

It *is* true. One day, North Hollywood Middle School had sent a letter home announcing that due to budget cuts, all extracurricular arts activities were being shut down.

We encourage kids to take advantage of the thriving arts community right here in the heart of North Hollywood! the letter had said.

Mom had shaken her head in disgust, ripping it up.

But what I'm not saying is how relieved I was not to have to audition for school plays.

I look at all their eyes, watching me.

"But even if you did, what?" DeSean asks.

I don't want to tell them how my heart starts to race in terror, just thinking about being on stage. Or how anxious I felt at the Kids' Cartoon Awards. I don't want to have to explain that I'd much rather be in the sound booth, where no one can see me.

"Musicals just aren't my thing!" I say. "Besides, I can't even sing!"

Monica crumples up her napkin. "Well, it's a *lot*

of fun. I'm trying out! I mean, we always do these old-school shows, like *Mary Poppins*. But who knows, maybe this year will be different!"

Mateo flips the cover of his sketchbook shut, but not before I catch a glimpse of his drawing. It's a skateboarder with a backward baseball cap, dressed in baggy pants that look just like Mateo's, his feet hovering over his board as he flies down a ramp. "I'm auditioning, too," he says. He raspberries his lips. "And I definitely can't sing." He unzips his book bag and slides his sketchbook into it. "Which means I'll be in the chorus. Where she puts all the non-singers. But"—he shrugs—"that's what I like. 'Cause if you mess up, no one notices."

"Wait, you're *all* auditioning for the musical?"

"Mm-hmm." DeSean nods.

"Does everyone at the school audition?"

Monica laughs. "No! Are you kidding me?" Then she arches an eyebrow and smiles. "Just the cool kids! Like us!"

I look out across the lunch room.

We're definitely *not* at the cool kids' table.

Which is perfectly fine by me.

Besides, would people think it's weird if I *wasn't* in the musical? Is Mateo right that if you can't sing, you just end up in the chorus?

Does that mean if I audition, I'd get to hang out with him . . . ?

Just as the bell rings, I hear myself saying, "I'll ask my mom about it tonight!"

CHAPTER 11

When I get home from school, Nana's napping like he usually is, and Mom has work to finish. Nani offers to make me a snack. "How about some homemade french fries?" She winks at me. "But made my special way. Give me a few minutes, okay?"

I head out to the back deck to let Streak run around and sniff for squirrels. He's pawing at the roots of the giant oak tree in the middle of the backyard when my phone rings.

It's Anton, video-calling me.

"Nikhiiiiiiiil!" He whisper-shouts as soon as I answer. His mouth takes up the entire phone screen. "Score! You're there!"

I laugh. "What are you doing? Aren't you in the middle of school right now?"

"Yup. But I got a bathroom pass, and now I'm hiding out in the boys' room. I'm definitely not supposed to be on my phone in here. I, like, one hundred percent could get detention right now."

He fans the phone back and forth to show me the inside of a bathroom stall. Then he spins it back around and I see him—fully clothed, thankfully—crouching on top of the toilet bowl.

"Remember this place?" he asks, wagging his eyebrows. "Bet you miss the scrumptious smell of the North Hollywood Middle School boys' room!"

He cracks up so hard at his own joke that it makes me laugh all over again.

I feel a tug of homesickness.

Not for the smell of farts, obviously.

But for my old school. And Anton.

"So?" His eyebrows hunker down, all serious. "Any good UFO sightings?"

"You'll be the first to know! I promise. But no. No UFO sightings. How are things over there?"

"*So* cool," he says, half lowering his eyelids. "So, so cool. I'm rocking the eighth grade!"

I imagine Anton, in the middle of his school day,

sneaking his phone out of his locker and running to the boys' room.

I wonder who he's hanging out with, now that I'm not there.

The sliding door opens and Nani pokes her head out. "Nikhil, beta? Whenever you're ready, the food is almost done."

"Okay, thanks, Nani." I watch Anton, not wanting to hang up just yet.

He bites his lip. "Before you go . . ." he says.

"Yeah?"

"I found out that parent-teacher conferences this year are right before Halloween weekend."

"Okay."

"Which means . . ."

"What?"

"It means . . . that we get an extra day off for Halloween."

"Really?" I feel another pang of sadness. Last year, I dressed up as the Mandalorian and Anton was Baby Yoda. His big green ears had kept running into, well, everything.

"Do you know what you're doing that weekend?" Anton asks. "Will you be in Ohio?"

"I think so? But I have no idea what I'm doing."

"Okay. Well. I was thinking. Well, my mom said she'd get me a plane ticket. Like, if you wanted me to come visit."

I stop in my tracks. "Wait. Really?"

"Only if it's okay with you. And like, with your mom, too," he says, and it seems like he's afraid I'm going to say no. But my whole heart wants to jump out of my body. "Of course it's okay! Are you kidding? I'll ask my mom tonight!"

And then he stands up on the toilet bowl and lifts both his arms up in the air. With the phone angled above him, I can see his whole body, from head to toe.

He screams at the top of his lungs, "WOOOOOOO-HOOOOOOOO!!!!! I'm going to Ohio!"

Then his face crumples, and we both hear a toilet flush. Someone mutters, "Well, lucky you."

The door to the boys' room slams shut.

Nani's already sitting at the dining table, reading a book and drinking a cup of tea, when I walk back in. Streak nudges the hem of her pants. "He's becoming quite my little buddy." She smiles.

She slides a bowl filled with hand-cut, deep-fried potato wedges toward me. Except they're lightly coated with red and brown spices.

I take a bite. "Wow. These are so good. Thanks, Nani."

"Has your mom made these for you? Masala fries?"

"I don't think so. Not like this."

I see her brow furrow ever so slightly. "Oh. But she cooks Indian food for you, right?"

"Yeah, of course." I reach for another french fry. "Why?"

Nani shakes her head. "No, no. I just . . . Nothing." She runs her hand along the front cover of her book.

The title is written in Gujarati.

"What's your book about?" I ask.

"Oh, this?" Her face lights up. "It's a book of poetry!" She flips it open and sets it down in front of me. "Can you read it?" she asks.

I shake my head. "I never learned how to. Read Gujarati, I mean," I say. "Or write it."

She frowns. "But you can speak it?"

"A little. Mom taught me a few words." I rest my hands on the table and sit up a little taller. "Kem cho, Nani?" I ask. It's a basic phrase that means "How are you?"

Nani smiles. "Hu majama." She claps. "Tane aatlu aude che thethi mane anand thayo." She answers me with "I'm good. If you even know this much, then I am happy."

"Mane pan gamyu," I say. It means "I like it, too."

"Arre vaah!" She heaps some praise on me.

I wish I could speak more with her, but I'm nervous I won't know enough other words, so instead I ask, "Do you read a lot, Nani?"

She gestures to the bookshelf in the living room. Every inch of it is filled with books. On some of the shelves, stacks of books are piled in front of the ones lined up behind them. It looks like they're fighting each other for space. Almost all the spines have Gujarati writing on them.

"Did you know your nani used to teach Gujarati literature? I have my master's degree in it!"

"Really? You're a teacher?"

"Well, I was. Back in India." Nani takes a sip of her tea. "But that was nearly fifty years ago!"

"Why did you stop?" I ask.

Nani peers at me over her teacup. "Are you really interested to know?"

I nod. And I am. I realize that I don't know much about Nani's life. At all.

"Well, when your nana and I immigrated to America, I wanted to keep teaching. I loved it so much! But none of the universities here offered classes in Gujarati literature. Nowadays, some schools have Hindi courses, but when we first arrived here, even that was unusual. So, I thought maybe I would teach some private lessons, find some students on my own. But there were so few Indian families living here at the time that there just wasn't any interest." Her face darkens, and her voice gets more serious. "Also, Nikhil, in those early years, when I would go to the grocery store, or try to make a deposit at the bank . . . well, sometimes people would look at me funny. Or laugh at my English. Or imitate my accent. Behind my back. Or even to my face. Once, somebody told me to go back to my own country. So, I was pretty sure they were not interested in learning my language."

She looks down at her hands resting in her lap, like she's thinking. And when she lifts her head back up, her eyes are twinkling. "There were so few Indian families in the area, in fact, that do you know how we made our first Indian friends here?"

"Unh-unh."

Nani suppresses a laugh. "Your nana and I got out the phone book and searched for anyone with common Indian last names. 'Shah,' like ours, or 'Patel,' and we would just give them a call! We found them in the phone book, can you imagine? You've probably never even seen a phone book!"

Now she leans back in her chair and lets herself have a real laugh. "And even though some of them lived half an hour away by car, to this day, they are our closest friends."

She gestures to the fries to remind me to eat. "Anyhow, this was a long way to say that there really weren't any students to teach when we first moved here."

"I'm sorry, Nani," I say. "Was that . . . hard for you?"

"Of course it was, beta." She puts her hand on my arm. "But there were so many other things I loved about living here! There were so many opportunities! Your nana was very busy back then, working at his engineering firm. And eventually, I took some other jobs myself. But then your mom was born. And I liked being at home to take care of her." She looks at the bookshelf like it holds something deeply powerful for her. "But of course I miss teaching."

She takes my face in the palms of her hands. "There are so many stories like mine. People who came to this country and had to reimagine their lives." She smiles. "I'm happy that you will know a little bit about my story."

Streak yips at our feet, trying to get in on all the love, and Nani quietly slips him a tiny piece of a french fry behind her back.

"Hey! No wonder he's your buddy!"

"Well, it's a nani's job to spoil her grandkids! And Streak is my second grandchild, right, Streak, beta?"

I laugh. Then, I'm not even sure why, but I set my hand on top of Nani's and squeeze it. "Thanks, Nani," I say. "For telling me all that."

CHAPTER 12

I'm sitting on my bed with my math homework laid out in front of me—Streak curled up in his own bed—when Mom knocks on my door.

"What are you working on there?" she asks.

"Algebra. It's the worst!" I groan.

"Want some help?"

"Sure. Can you tell me what a polynomial is?"

Mom looks over my shoulder at my laptop. Then she pats my back. "Well. I wouldn't want to deprive you from learning. I'm sure you'll figure it out."

She sits down next to me and runs her hand along the tulip-patterned comforter on my bed. "You wanted to talk to me?" she asks. But before I can answer, she adds, "We should get you some things to make this bedroom your own, huh? Want to go shopping this weekend?"

"Yeah! Can I get some glow-in-the-dark stars for the ceiling? Or a *Minecraft* poster?"

She smiles. "Strong choices! I think I can make that happen." She pats my arm. "So, what's up?"

I have a couple things I need to ask Mom, so I start with the easiest. "Would it be okay if Anton came to visit for Halloween? His parents said they'd buy him a plane ticket, if it was all right with you."

"They did? Yes, of course! I think that's a great idea. I'll call his mom tomorrow."

I feel an excitement building inside me. "Cool! Have you heard of a place called Wright-Patterson Air Force Base? Can we take him there? As a surprise?" I waggle my eyebrows. "There have been alien sightings there!"

Mom cocks her head at me. Then she forms an O with her lips. "I remember those alien rumors from when I was a kid! Yes, we can go there! It's not far from here. Are you guys gonna get dressed up this year? Did you discuss Halloween costumes?"

"We didn't, but I can ask him!" I'm getting so pumped that I almost stumble onto my next question.

"Can I also audition for the school musical?" It comes out faster than I expect it to, and almost immediately my stomach starts churning. "I mean, I'd have to go to after-school rehearsals"—I try to play it off—"so it probably won't even work. You know, with *RROS* and all."

"I think that's a terrific idea!" She almost cuts me off. Then she starts singing our favorite song from *The Greatest Showman*, the one we sang on repeat for five days on our never-ending road trip. She throws her head back and belts, "I am not a stranger to the dark!"

"No, Mom! No 'This Is Me'! No 'This Is Me'!" I wave my arms back and forth in front of her face.

She laughs. "Nikhil, I'm so glad you're getting involved in your school already. And don't worry about the recording schedule. We'll work it out with Josh, okay?"

"Okay." I scratch the front of my jeans. I think part of me was hoping she'd say no, even though I guess I knew she wouldn't.

My last question feels the hardest, but it's been stuck inside my head ever since I had french fries with Nani. "Mom." I swallow. "Do you and Nana just not get along? Or did something happen? I mean, why haven't we visited in all these years?"

Concern passes over her face. "What makes you ask?"

"I don't know. I just. I was talking to Nani today. About how she used to teach. And . . . well, I guess I realized that I don't know that much about our family. I was wondering why."

Mom clears her throat. "Well, it's pretty complicated, Nikhil. But . . . first of all, I hope you know that this isn't about your nani. I love her very much. And I love your nana, too. But I'm sure you see how he and I can get with each other. We don't see eye to eye on a lot of things. And it's been like that for years."

"Right. But . . . did something happen to make it that way?"

She takes a breath. "Yes, Nikhil," she says. "Something did." She pauses. "I haven't talked to you about these things because you're still young. But"—she presses her hand against my cheek—"I guess you're growing up, huh?"

I nod, waiting for her to go on.

"So, Nani told you that she was a teacher? Back in India?"

"Mm-hmm."

"Okay. Well, let's start there. When your nana and nani got married back in India, your nana liked that she was a teacher—that she was educated, and had a job and a career. But when they moved here . . . well, I don't think he understood how hard it was for her to give that up. When he got busy at work, he thought that she should be happy staying at home while he went to the office."

"But . . . I thought Nani couldn't teach anyway? Right? And that she liked being home to take care of you."

"That's right," Mom says. But now she takes my arm, like she really wants me to understand what she's saying. "But it's more Nana's attitude that I'm talking about. In a lot of ways, he has a more traditional way of thinking about things. He thinks that women—even if they have a job—should prioritize taking care of their families, and men should focus on their careers. And that's not fair."

Mom looks down at the bed and gathers her thoughts.

"And he treated me the same way. See, he supported me studying and wanted me to work. But he also thought it was important I start a family. Maybe it was the way he was brought up. Maybe he thought he was doing what was best. I don't know. But he put a lot of pressure on me to get married. To find a husband. And that was hard. Because that's not what I wanted at the time. But somewhere, deep down"—she shakes her head—"I also wanted to make your nana happy. He's my dad, after all."

She hesitates again. Like she's checking to make sure that I can handle this.

But I don't want her to stop. "So, what happened?" I ask.

"Well, I married your dad. To please Nana, mostly. But, Nikhil, it was a mistake! Your dad and I weren't a good match. We got married too quickly. And shortly after you were born, we realized we weren't happy together. So, we decided to get divorced. Well, that upset your nana, too. He thought we should try harder to make it work. He thought divorce would bring shame to the family. Ruin his reputation. He was really hard on me."

Mom looks up over my head, and it's almost like she's reliving the past.

"Anyway. After we got divorced, and your dad got remarried and moved to Texas, I said, maybe it's time I tried things *my* way. Maybe it's time to build my life, the way *I* want to." She takes my hand. "And that's when you and I moved to Los Angeles."

There are crease lines in Mom's forehead, and I can tell that she's worried that maybe she's said too much. I want to let her know that it's okay. So, I say, "Mom? Have you ever told Nana to just stop telling you what to do?"

She leans in and kisses the top of my head. Then she smiles and pulls me into her. "That's a good idea, Nikhil. A very good idea."

That night, I duck down under the covers.

I turn on my phone, and—even though I'm not supposed to watch TV this late—I look for an old episode of *The Loud House* or *Bunk'd*.

I flip through a couple cartoons, but they don't seem to slow all the thoughts racing through my mind like they usually do. So, I open up the *RROS* Instagram account. Most of the posts are images from the show, mixed in with a few videos of me and some of the rest of the cast. I scroll through the comments.

utahgal101 I wanna be Raj Reddy when I grow up 🖤🖤🖤🖤
jfrombraxil You guys are da bomba! 💥💥

I think about Nani and how much she loves her books. And I think about Mom, and how happy she was when she started her own company.

I swipe my thumb along the screen of my phone, watching all the posts and comments fly by.

I can't imagine if Mom hadn't let me audition for this.

CHAPTER 13

Auditions for the musical come sooner than I was hoping for.

I thought I'd be the only one who was a complete mess, but when I meet up with DeSean, Monica, and Mateo in the hallway outside the auditorium, it's clear that we're all a bundle of nerves.

DeSean's arms are up over his head, and he's shaking his hands back and forth, hard. Monica's pacing next to him, stretching her face as wide as she can and then scrunching it up.

I'm just about to spin on my heels and call the whole thing off when Mateo sees me. He flips his hair back and waves. I try to say, "Hey!" but the tension makes my voice come out higher than I expect it to. It makes everyone burst out laughing, and for a moment, all our anxiety melts away.

We push open the double doors to the auditorium and make our way down the center aisle. Kids are already piling into the orange-fabric-covered seats that fan out on either side of us. I walk past a girl in pigtails. She nudges the kid next to her. Then she points at me and whispers. A boy with freckles cranes his neck so far in my direction that he almost falls out of his chair.

My breath comes in fast and shallow. Why am I doing this? I'm going to have to sing. In front of all these people.

Mrs. Reed walks briskly out onto the stage. She flaps the toes of her shoes along the floor like a tap dancer, and then she glides two fingers up the keys of the piano. "Welcome one and welcome all! Hello, my little storytellers!" She spins around and grabs a marker from the tray under the whiteboard behind her. She scrawls the word "AUDITIONS!" across it in bright purple. "Today's a big da-ay!" she singsongs, before spinning back around.

The four of us duck down into the second row and stuff our backpacks under our chairs. I swivel my head and look at the back of the auditorium.

The Exit sign. It's still there.

"As you all know, this year, we'll be doing a revue of some of the greatest shows on Broadway, so there will be plenty of parts for everyone. But there is one lead character, who'll be written by yours truly!" Mrs. Reed raises her arm in a flourish over her head. "The Narrator!" She shields her eyes from the stage lights and scans the auditorium. Her gaze lands on the four of us.

I peek at DeSean. He's listening intently.

"So, let's all get up here. I'll teach you some music, and then everyone will get a chance to sing, okay?"

I force myself to climb up the four short steps that lead up to the stage with the rest of the kids. DeSean motions for me to join him at the front, near the piano, but I pretend to get stuck behind a group of kids. I drift to the back. My palms are sweating. A boy next to me taps my arm. "So, I guess you'll be playing the Narrator, huh?" he says.

"What? No, I don't think so." I try not to sound panicked. "I'm pretty sure it'll be DeSean. Won't it?"

He looks confused. "But you're, like, on TV."

Mateo slides in next to me, his hands stuffed in his pockets, and I do my best not to notice him.

Mrs. Reed bangs out a tune on the piano. I hum the whole song under my breath, terrified. I'm sure I sound awful.

We run through it a few times as a group, and then Mrs. Reed calls us up one by one.

With every kid who takes their turn, my anxiety only grows.

Monica goes, and she's really good. She casually throws in some killer dance moves, one elbow up over her head and a knee hiked in the air. She smiles proudly and mouths, "Nailed it!" when she's done. Mateo's right after her. He speak-sings the whole song, and then takes a bow when he finishes, bending one leg back behind the other, like a curtsy. "Thank you," he whispers. It's so unexpected, it makes me smile.

And then it's DeSean's turn.

He plants his feet firmly on the ground and looks up at the back row of the audience. A hush falls over all of us, and I can almost picture him on a Broadway stage. He starts softly. Then he riffs on a few of the notes, getting louder as he goes. And finally, he stretches out both his hands and finishes the song a *whole octave* higher than Mrs. Reed taught us!

It's amazing. There's even some applause when he's done.

"And now for our young professional, Nik-heeee-uuuul! Come on up!" Mrs. Reed plays the first four bars over and over. I glance back at the Exit sign.

"Get it, Reddy!" someone bellows, their hands cupped over their mouth.

I yank on the front of my T-shirt and make my way up to the piano. I look at Mrs. Reed. It feels like her face is two miles away from me. I turn back to the other kids.

There's a really good chance that I'm going to throw up.

The first few lines of the verse we're singing is from the opening number that Mrs. Reed wrote for the Narrator.

So, take my hand!
Hold on tight!
You're in for a real
Treat tonight!

It's not meant to be funny.
But when I play Raj Reddy, that's what I get to do.

And I know how to pitch my voice up to make things even funnier.

Mrs. Reed plays the first chord.

"So, take my hand!" I sing, coming in a little too quickly. One of the notes is wrong, but without even thinking, I stretch my palm toward the kid in the front row. I beckon at him with my pointer finger. Then I wink, and it makes all the kids around him chuckle. "Hold on tight!" I scream-sing, pitching my voice up just so. I fling myself to the ground in a pratfall, acting like I'm on a raft in the middle of the ocean and I'm being dunked by a giant wave. More kids start laughing. Then I hop up onto my knees and shake off the imaginary water. I reach up, like I'm fighting to pull myself out of the ocean. "You're in for a real treat . . . !" The notes are all over the place, but I'm giving it my all. Finally, I leap up to my feet and fling my arms to the side, shaking my fingers like tambourines. "Toniiiiight!"

Everyone is roaring. But in a good way! Mrs. Reed stands up at the piano. "Well, that's not what I thought that song was about. At all! But way to work the audience! Kids, I hope you were paying attention!"

I look out to see Monica clapping. Mateo's grin is even wider than normal.

DeSean's in the front row. I flip my palms up and bite my lip. I mouth, "What just happened?"

He laughs.

But I see something else on his face, too.

It's an expression I can't quite read.

CHAPTER 14

"**R**umor has it that Mrs. Reed is finally posting the cast list after school today!" Monica is standing at my locker, rocking back and forth in her Doc Martens.

"Really? So soon?" I tug on the string of my maroon hoodie. The fall in Ohio is cooler than it is in LA, but right now I feel heat creeping up the back of my neck. I try to shove away the nagging feeling that auditioning for the musical was a bad idea.

"*Soon?*" Monica looks at me like I'm being absurd. "I feel like we've been waiting forever! It's been two whole weeks!"

Ever since the auditions, we've all congratulated

each other on just getting through them, but anytime someone would laugh about how funny I was—or even mention the word "Narrator"—I'd stick my tongue out and face-palm myself, saying, "Too bad it's a musical! Which means you have to sing!"

DeSean *has* to get the Narrator, right? I mean, Mrs. Reed told him this was going to be his year! In front of me. On the first day of school.

"Want to meet outside her classroom after school to see if the list's up?" Monica asks.

"Sure!" I try to act as excited as she is.

As she heads down the hallway, I call after her, "Fingers crossed we all got great parts!"

The entire day, I concentrate as hard as I can on my work. In English, I bury my head in *Look Both Ways*; in science I take notes on the difference between elements, compounds, and pure substances; in history, I pretend to be fascinated as Mr. Cooper drones on and on about the Battle of Antietam.

But no matter how hard I will it not to, the last bell of the day finally rings.

Like a siren.

I trudge down the hallway to Mrs. Reed's classroom.

A kid heading in the opposite direction cups

his hands around his mouth and yells, "RAAAAJ REDDDYYYY! Can't wait to hear you sing, dude!"

I feel the backs of my ears turn red.

The girl walking next to him nudges him. "His name's Nikhil, right? It's not actually Raj Reddy, is it?"

I pull my hoodie up over my head and scooch past them as quickly as I can.

A group of kids is already crowded around the window next to Mrs. Reed's door.

I see Monica and Mateo in the back, whispering to each other, a look of concern on their faces.

I step up to the group. I peek between two kids' heads and try to see the list.

There, at the top, in bold-face type, I read:

NARRATOR: Nikhil Shah

My stomach dips. Fast and hard.

Just below my name, I see DeSean's, with a few song titles typed in below it. Monica's name is just under that.

But everything else goes blurry.

"Hey." Someone taps my back, and I spin around. It's DeSean. "Congratulations," he says, even though he sounds a bit deflated. "I had a feeling you'd get the lead."

My shoulders have somehow managed to climb all the way up to my ears. "I . . . Really? I was sure it would be y—"

"Nikhil?" Kyle, the kid who I met in the cafeteria, pushes his way through the crowd. "Remember me? From newspaper? Can we still do that interview? It'll be even better now! We can make it all about how the star of *RROS* is going to be the lead in the musical! This has got to be a Sycamore first!"

DeSean pats my shoulder. "Well, I gotta run. Voice lesson," he says.

I try to go after him, but Kyle blocks my way. "So, when's good for you?" he asks. "Maybe one day at lunch? Or during study hall?"

"Whenever!" I yell, pushing past him. "Just find me whenever you want, okay?"

But by the time I get to the parking lot, DeSean is already climbing into the back seat of his minivan. Two women, who I guess are his moms, are in the front. I see one of them turn around to talk to him as they pull out of the carpool line.

I watch the back of his car get smaller and smaller as they drive off.

I wonder if they're asking him about the cast list.

CHAPTER 15

A profile pic of an illustrated space helmet pops up next to Anton 's screen name.

AntsyCosmonaut: Wait. I'm confused. Tell me again. Why aren't you happy about this?

I type in my response:

RajReddy's_EvilTwin: Because! The Narrator's the lead, and the lead should have gone to DeSean! He can sing! Like, for real!

I jiggle my legs, swiveling in Mom's desk chair, waiting for Anton to respond. Streak cocks his ear at me from his dog bed.

It's Sunday afternoon, and Mom's convinced Nana that they should visit a family friend. While they're gone, she said I could use her computer to play *Minecraft*.

The game's on the center screen, in creative mode, and Anton and I are chatting on the monitor on my right.

Footsteps thump around upstairs, echoing through the basement ceiling. Nana groans and mutters something I can't hear. "It'll be good for you to get out of the house, Dad!" Mom answers, frustrated. "Besides, in a few months you'll complain that it's too cold out!"

"They'll be happy to see you after so long, Deepa!" Nani pipes in. "We've known Ramesh and Hansa Patel since before you were born!"

Mom calls down the basement stairs, "Nikhil! Time limit on the video games, okay?"

And then, the front door slams shut.

Anton adds a barrier block to the top of the *Minecraft* waterfall we're constructing.

Finally, a text pops up.

AntsyCosmonaut: Well, you both auditioned and YOU got the part! Besides, of course you're the lead! YOU'RE the great Raj Reddy!

I furrow my brow.

RajReddy's_EvilTwin: Right, but . . . you know how nervous I get being on stage! And the Narrator has FOUR SONGS! I should never have auditioned in the first place! This was a terrible idea!

I add three more blocks to the trench that I'm building. It's going to form a lake, to keep the waterfall from overflowing.

AntsyCosmonaut: Well, why *did* you then?

I swallow, thinking about Anton's question.

RajReddy's_EvilTwin: I don't know! Just forget it! What's going on over there, anyhow?

There's a long pause, then Anton writes:

AntsyCosmonaut: This is really weird. But do you

remember Melissa? Roper?

RajReddy's_EvilTwin: Um. Yeah. Of course I do.

Last year, Melissa Roper would barely give us the time of day. The one time she *did* say hi, it was to stop us in the hall so she could get a selfie with me. Anton had done this strange bow and said, "I'd be happy to take the picture for you, m'lady!" Which was already weird. But then he tripped on his shoelace and dropped her phone on the ground.

Her phone was fine, but Melissa never did get that selfie.

AntsyCosmonaut: Well, she's having a birthday party. And she invited me.

He builds out more of the barrier.

RajReddy's_EvilTwin: Really?

Then I ask:

RajReddy's_EvilTwin: When is it?
AntsyCosmonaut: Why does that even matter? I'm not going!

I twist my lips to the side.

RajReddy's_EvilTwin: Why not? She invited you, right?

AntsyCosmonaut: Right! But why? I've barely ever spoken to her!

I'm not sure what to write, so I don't say anything. Half a second goes by, before I get:

AntsyCosmonaut: Anyway, guess what?

RajReddy's_EvilTwin: ??

AntsyCosmonaut: My mom bought my plane ticket! She emailed your mom the flight times.

RajReddy's_EvilTwin: I know! My mom told me! Sweet!

AntsyCosmonaut: Will we, like, go trick-or-treating? Should we get costumes?

RajReddy's_EvilTwin: Oh yeah! I meant to ask you about that. We should definitely get costumes!

AntsyCosmonaut: What should we go as?

RajReddy's_EvilTwin: Um. Famous outer space duos that we haven't already been . . . go!

I rack my brain for ideas while I keep building out the trench.

AntsyCosmonaut: Should we go classic? Like R2-D2 and C-3PO?

RajReddy's_EvilTwin: Oh! Nice!

I'm about to ask Anton about Melissa again, but he has more questions.

AntsyCosmonaut: So, what's the trick-or-treating like there?

RajReddy's_EvilTwin: I'm not sure. But I can ask around.

There's a slight pause, and then he writes.

AntsyCosmonaut: Ask, like, who?

RajReddy's_EvilTwin: I dunno. Just my new friends. At school.

There's another pause.

AntsyCosmonaut: Oh, cool.

Then:

AntsyCosmonaut: Would they, like, come with us?

RajReddy's_EvilTwin: Maybe? To be honest, I'm not sure how DeSean feels about me right now. But they're all super nice. I mean, the reason I auditioned for the musical in the first place was because they all were.

I consider telling him about Mateo.

But for some reason, I hesitate.

Not because Anton would have a problem with it. He wouldn't.

I mean, Anton was the second person in the world who I came out to. Right after Mom. And he was really cool about it. In fact, everyone I cared about was, including Josh.

But even though Anton knows I'm gay, it's not like we sit around talking about it. Besides, I don't even know if Mateo likes boys!

AntsyCosmonaut: Huh. Okay. Well. They sound fun.

Something about the tone of his text feels off to me. I stare at the computer screen. I look back at the last few messages. Does Anton *not* want to meet my new friends here?

And why did he bring up Melissa's party in the first place, just to tell me he isn't going?

I chew my lip, trying to figure out why things seem so weird.

Then, I write:

RajReddy's_EvilTwin: Honestly, we might not even have time to trick-or-treat anyway. Not with all the ALIEN STUFF we have to do!

His response flies in.

AntsyCosmonaut: What do you mean alien stuff?
RajReddy's_EvilTwin: 👻. I'm just saying. It *is* Ohio after all.
AntsyCosmonaut: Wait, Nikhil. Seriously? What are you talking about?

But instead of answering him, I add the last block to my trench.

RajReddy's_EvilTwin: Are we going to test out this waterfall before my mom gets home or what?

Before he can respond, I press the command blocks, and bright blue water comes crashing down over his barrier and into my lake.

AntsyCosmonaut: WHOA! IT'S AWESOME!

Then he writes:

AntsyCosmonaut: Seriously, what alien stuff?

But there's no way I'm telling him that Mom's taking us to Wright-Patterson Air Force Base. It's too good of a surprise.

Now that our conversation feels back to normal, I type:

RajReddy's_EvilTwin: If I were you, I'd go to Melissa's party. Who knows? It might be fun.

I wait for what feels like forever.

AntsyCosmonaut: Yeah? Well, if I were you, I'd stop worrying about the musical. You know you'll rock it! You always do!

I hear the sound of the garage door opening, and I quickly power down Mom's computer and dart up the stairs. How did the time go by so fast? I throw myself on the sofa and flip open my laptop, acting like I'm engrossed in my schoolwork.

But Anton's words rattle around in my head.

Maybe he's right.

Maybe I can rock this musical.

CHAPTER 16

On the first day of rehearsals, I'm running late for school.

Mom's already in the car, honking the horn like a warning signal. Nani's in the dining room, getting Nana his breakfast. I dart past them and grab my lunch bag off the table. I'm halfway out the door when Nani calls, "Don't I get a goodbye?"

I spin around and wave, yelling, "Bye, Naniiii!" when the "ee" of Nani slides up high, then back down, and finally lands on something that sounds like three different notes jangling around in the back of my throat.

What was *that*?

The whole way to school, I quietly swallow and clear my throat, hoping that there's just something stuck back there.

But, of course, there isn't.

As soon as Mom drops me off, I beeline it for the boys' room. I dip down to check under the stalls. No one.

I look at myself in the mirror.

"Hello. Hellooooo. Hullo. Hi."

I say it over and over again.

Every time, I sound completely normal.

I pitch my voice up. "I'm Raj Reddy," I say.

It sounds exactly the way it always does.

Doesn't it?

By the time lunch rolls around, I've worked myself into a frenzy.

I spend most of history with my phone hidden under my desk, googling, "What happens when your voice starts to change?" and "Child actors whose voices crack" on my phone.

But no matter how many websites I read—with embarrassing titles like "Puberty Is Your Friend," and "Ready or Not, Here Comes Puberty!"—they all tell me what I already know.

Once it starts, you can't stop it.

And actors whose voices change get replaced by other actors. With non-cracking voices.

Ever since I got cast as Raj Reddy, somewhere in the back of my head I've known that it wouldn't last forever. I mean, I'm well aware of how many actors have played Lincoln Loud on *The Loud House*. A lot! *Because* their voices started cracking! And Lincoln Loud is twelve, just like Raj.

But still. I'm not ready for this to happen.

Not *now*.

I thought I'd have at least until I was fourteen. Or fifteen, if I was lucky!

I push open the doors to the cafeteria. I'm about to head over to our usual table when Kyle from newspaper steps in front of me.

"Nikhil? It's Kyle. From newspaper. Can we do that interview now?"

"Oh, um." I peer over at our table. "Really? Like, right now? I mean, can't I have, like, a couple days to prepare for it or something?"

Kyle's face drops. "Aw, come on! You said whenever! If we do it today, I can still get it into this week's paper! Otherwise I'll have to wait, like, a whole month for the next edition." He looks up at me hopefully. "Please? I've been working on my questions forever!"

"Right, I just . . ." At our table, I see Monica, DeSean, and Mateo. They're laughing. Which is something the four of us haven't been doing much of the last several days.

It seems like ever since the cast list went up, our conversations have been totally awkward. I feel like I'm walking on eggshells, doing everything I can to avoid talking about the show. Monica and Mateo are trying to act happy I got the lead, but I can tell that they don't want to make DeSean feel bad either. And it's pretty clear that DeSean is doing his best to hide how disappointed he is.

So, the four of us kind of just sit there. Talking about nothing.

I turn back to Kyle. "Um. You know what? Sure."

I realize that I've been running my thumb back and forth along the side of my throat the whole time we've been standing here, even though my voice hasn't cracked once since seven thirty this morning.

I pull out a chair across from him.

"All righty," he begins, wiping his blond hair

out of his eyes. He hits the Voice Record button on his phone. "Tell me everything about playing Raj Reddy!"

That's the question he's been working on? *Forever?*

I tell him all the same things I've ever said in interviews before. That I've loved cartoons since I was really little. That there were, like, a million callbacks. That getting to be in the sound booth is a dream come true, and that I had no idea the show would be this popular.

I tell him that it feels really good knowing that I make people laugh.

Then Kyle says, "And now you're the lead of the musical! Are you excited about it?"

"Um . . ." I clear my throat subconsciously. "Yes! Of course! I think . . . You know, I think it's gonna be a lot of fun. First rehearsal's today! So . . . We'll see!"

Kyle leans forward. "I'm pretty sure this year, *everyone's* going to be coming to the show. I mean, I know I am. And I didn't step foot anywhere near the musical in sixth grade *or* seventh grade. It isn't exactly a hot ticket around here."

"Oh. It's not?"

"Nope! Okay, last question. It's your first year at Sycamore. A couple of girls in our grade . . ." He giggles. "Well, they're wondering if you have a girl-friend in Los Angeles? Or . . . would it be okay if one of them asks you out?"

"If one of them . . . ? Wait, is this for the paper?" I glance down at his phone.

"Yeah. Why not?"

"Oh, um." I rub the front of my jeans. "Well . . ." Out of the corner of my eye, I see Mateo stand up. He slides his sketchbook into his backpack and picks up his tray.

I'm not sure I want to talk about this in the paper. But I definitely don't want to lie about it either.

Kyle shifts to the edge of his seat.

"I don't have a girlfriend, but . . ."

"But?"

"Well, even if I did . . . I guess what I'm trying to say is . . . Well, let's just say, it wouldn't be a girl." I realize that I'm clenching my hand.

Kyle bites his thumbnail. "Wouldn't be a . . . ? Ohhhhhh, wait. Like, you mean . . . you're gay?"

"Um . . . yeah."

"Huh." A look of surprise passes over Kyle's face.

But then the corners of his mouth turn up. "That's cool. I just didn't know. Sorry. I didn't mean to assume."

I shrug.

"Is it okay if I put that in the paper?" he asks.

Mateo's standing by the trash cans. He picks up the milk carton off his tray. He lowers his nose toward it and sniffs. Then—even though I'm pretty sure he has no idea anyone is watching him—he sticks his tongue out and pretends to gag.

It makes me laugh.

"Um, sure, you can put that in the paper," I say.

By the time the last bell of the day rings, my voice hasn't cracked for hours.

Even so, I find myself trudging toward first rehearsal. When I get to the auditorium, everybody else is already there.

I sneak into the last row.

"Well, look who's here! Our Narrator's finally arrived!" Mrs. Reed calls out from where she's standing on the stage. She bangs out an ominous-sounding chord on the piano. "I thought maybe you weren't joining us!" She chuckles to herself, and then she clutches her chest dramatically. "I thought maybe the world of for-profit television had stolen you away from the live theater!" She says "live theater" like she's in a Shakespeare play and she's the queen of England. A few kids in the front row laugh. She peers over the stage at them. "Thank you! I'm here all week!

"All right! Let's all gather around the piano!" She flaps her shoe against the stage. Even though she still isn't wearing tap shoes. "To kick things off, I thought, what better way to break the ice than to just dive right into the opening number!"

The *what*?

"No pressure to get anything right. It's only the first day. We'll just have a little fun with the music! But since this song is all about the magic of the theater"—she says "theater" in that British accent again—"I thought it'd be the perfect way to kick off rehearsals! We'll sing it through once, and then we can chat about what it means after!"

I feel a tightening sensation in my chest that threatens to cut off the flow of oxygen to the rest of my body.

The opening number is all about the Narrator. *Why* would we start with this? I thought the first day would be just about sitting around and getting to know each other!

I follow everyone up onto the stage and grab some sheet music from the stack of papers that are being passed around.

I step in next to DeSean.

"Hey," I whisper.

"Hey," he says. "What's up?"

But now I'm not sure what to say. "Um . . ."

He watches me, waiting for me to go on.

"Sorry. About lunch," I say. "I wanted to sit with you guys, but I had to do that interview for the school paper."

As soon as it comes out of my mouth, I wish I could take it back. It should have been *him* being interviewed about the musical.

But there's no time to even think about apologizing, because now Mrs. Reed is waving me up to the front. "Since you sing the first few verses solo, Nikhil, why don't you stand up here by me? I'll let the rest of the group know where to come in for the chorus. And then we'll all sing together!"

I make my way up to the piano bench.

I look at the music in my hands. *You can do this,* I

tell myself. *Just be funny, like you were at the auditions.*

But somehow, this feels different.

I feel . . . naked. Or something. Like I can't hide.

Mrs. Reed bangs out the opening notes. "Remember the tune?" She sings the first few lines. Her voice is loud and clear.

I nod.

"Great! Here we go!" She plays the beginning chord, and I take a deep breath.

I start singing softly, and Mrs. Reed smiles at me encouragingly. I'm halfway through the third line when she joins in with me, but it feels like we're singing two different songs. My notes don't match hers, and she's singing it a lot slower than I am.

Am I going too fast?

I force myself to peek up at the rest of the cast.

Why are they looking at me like that? Am I that bad?

I slam my eyes shut. But now I can't see my music.

Instead, I see the faces of the rest of the kids. They're inside my head, laughing. Uncontrollably. At me.

"Hang on!" I hold out both my hands. I spin around to face Mrs. Reed. "What's happening? Are you singing too slow, or am I going too fast?"

As I say the word "fast" the "aa" gets squeezed inside my throat. I sound like a chipmunk.

Mrs. Reed's eyebrows stretch up over her glasses.

I'm expecting her to double over.

I'm expecting everyone to.

But instead, it's like no one's even noticed.

"It's okay, Nikhil," Mrs. Reed says. "You were singing *a little* over tempo there, but it's just the first day!"

Someone snickers, and it sounds like they say, "Were those even the right notes?"

Mrs. Reed must see something written across my face, because she rests both of her hands on the piano. "Everyone! I thought that was an amazing start! What can we all learn from Nikhil?"

She looks out at twenty expectant faces.

"On the very first day," she goes on, "he dove right in! Fearlessly! And that's what the theater is all about!"

I look down at the stage.

That wasn't fearless. I was terrified.

I'm praying that Mrs. Reed won't make me do it again. I can't risk my voice cracking. To my surprise, she closes the lid of the piano and says, "You know what? Since it's only the first day, why don't we play some theater games to shake things up? Who wants to kick us off in a game of Zip-Zap-Zop?"

CHAPTER 17

The tension between DeSean, Monica, Mateo, and me only grows.

Except now I'm pretty sure it's not just 'cause I'm the lead, but because they all know that I've been horribly miscast, too.

In math class, I try to arrive early and pick a desk between two that are already taken, just so I won't have to sit next to Monica or DeSean. And I have a feeling DeSean might be doing the same thing.

When I walk Streak in the neighborhood, I keep one eye on the lookout for him, even though I still don't know which house is his.

Lunch is the only time the four of us are forced to be alone together. It'd just be too obvious if we suddenly sat at different tables. But the hour has gotten so painfully quiet that I find myself wishing I could be like Mateo. At least he has his sketchbook to disappear into.

If there was a way to rewind and never have auditioned for the musical in the first place, I would.

But there isn't.

And then, a few days later, it's officially in print.

"Free copies of *The Monthly Prairie Dog!*" Kyle's standing on the sidewalk in front of school as Mom pulls into the carpool line. He has a stack of folded-up newspapers in his hand. "First edition of the year! Get 'em while they're hot off the press!" He's really leaning into his paperboy role.

I try to exit Mom's car as quickly as possible. But my seatbelt gets stuck in the clasp. I yank on it. It won't budge. Kyle waves a newspaper at a girl walking by him. She makes a face at him. "Isn't all this paper bad for the environment?"

"What are you talking about?" He throws his head back in faux disgust. "It's print journalism at its finest!" He dangles the paper under her nose.

"But if you're so against paper, you can read it online."

"Wait, is that the Raj Reddy guy on the front?" She grabs for the paper. "I'll take one."

I'm swinging my legs out of the car when Kyle comes running over. "Nikhil! Thank you so much! My mom is going to flip!" He leans against the door-jamb. "Guess who got the cover story?"

There, on the front fold of the paper, is a photograph of me next to a screen grab of Raj Reddy. Block letters announce: "FROM OUTER SPACE TO THE SYCAMORE STAGE!" Underneath, in slightly smaller letters, it says, *All the secrets you've ever wanted to know about the star of* RROS.

"Oh. Wow. Congrats, Kyle," I say.

Mom leans over and stretches her arm out. She wriggles her fingers. "Nikhil, why didn't you tell me about this? I'm going to need one of those! And can I get an extra for Nikhil's grandparents?"

"Really? You want *my* interview? You must have a million articles about Nikhil!" Kyle proudly hands her two copies before dropping one in my lap.

I scoot out of the car. "Well! We should get going." I stick the paper under my arm. "Don't want to be late for class!" I walk casually down the sidewalk until Mom's car is gone. Then I make a mad dash for my locker. But I only get to read the first paragraph before the bell rings. I stuff the paper deep inside my book bag. As far down as I can.

In English, I get asked to sign about five copies of *The Monthly Prairie Dog.* In science, a kid pats me on the back and says, "Way to go, man." Another gives me a thumbs-up.

By the time history rolls around, Mr. Cooper makes everyone hand their papers up so he can pile them in a stack on his desk. "Nikhil will sign these *after* class is over," he says. "Now can we all focus on the Great Depression, please?"

And when I walk into the cafeteria for lunch, the whole room erupts in applause.

I'm not sure how to respond, so I raise one hand up to the middle of my chest and give everyone a half wave. Which only elicits more applause. I can't get to our table soon enough.

I slide into my usual seat and let out a huge breath. "What is going on?"

Mateo brushes his hair out of his eyes and peeks

up at me. We make eye contact, and his cheeks turn the faintest hint of red before he quickly stares down at his sketchbook again.

"Wait, for real? Why is everyone clapping for me?" I look at Monica and DeSean.

Monica reaches across the table and rests her hand on my arm. "I think everyone just thinks it's really cool. I don't think anyone's ever said that in our school newspaper before."

DeSean sets his spoon down. "It *is* really cool." He says it so genuinely that it makes me want to kick myself for how weird I've been being lately.

I reach for the folded-up paper next to Mateo's lunchbox.

I skim past the first couple paragraphs. There's definitely a lot of fan-boying. Kyle mentions all his favorite episodes and brags about the lines he can quote by heart. Then toward the bottom of the page, I read:

> And if you didn't think Nikhil was awesome just for being the voice of one of the best cartoon characters on TV ever, check this out—he also told me that I could put in the paper that he's

gay! Which, if you ask me, is pretty brave of him. Is there anything this kid can't do?

I'm warning you, reserve your tickets to the musical now, because they're going to go fast!

And oh, in case anyone's wondering, he doesn't have a boyfriend. Yet.

I stare at the paper.

Right.

I told Kyle I was gay. I've been so stressed about the musical, I almost forgot.

I've never seen that word—"gay"—next to my name in print. It feels so, I don't know . . . public.

"You okay, Nikhil?" Monica asks.

"Uh-huh," I say.

"Wait a minute," she says slowly. "You *are* gay, right?"

DeSean eyes me, warily. "You gave him permission to write that, didn't you? I mean, he didn't out you, did he?"

"No! No. I mean, yes! I am. And yes, I told him he could put it in the paper."

"Oh, good." Monica breathes a sigh of relief. "The look on your face had me worried there!" Then she adds, "I agree with Kyle. It is really brave of you."

"Thanks," I mutter.

I glance at Mateo.

He's still focused on his sketchbook, but his pencil isn't moving.

As I'm heading to my locker after lunch, Mateo catches up to me.

"Nikhil?" He chews on the corner of his lip.

"Yeah?"

He stretches the front of his hoodie away from his waist, his fists buried deep inside the pockets.

"I . . ." He kicks the toe of his Vans against the floor. "I just . . ."

The bell for the next period rings. He glances at the clock hanging over the row of lockers, but neither of us moves.

Then the words come flying out of his mouth. "I just wanted to tell you . . . I'm gay, too. And I don't think I could ever say that in a newspaper! I mean, I haven't even told my parents yet! I mean, Monica knows. And I'm pretty sure DeSean knows, but . . . that's it. So . . ." His face reddens. "I don't know why, but I just wanted to tell you that!"

And then before I can even catch my breath, he darts off.

I freeze. I watch everyone run to get to class on time.

So, Mateo is gay.

That's cool.

CHAPTER 18

After school, I have to record on *RROS*.

"All right, we're on line 182. Give me three takes in a row." Josh's voice trickles into my headphones.

This week's episode is about a wise old alien named Dobrink. Even though he's lived for thousands of years, he still needs Raj's help. And just before Raj leaves his planet, Dobrink says, "Age shouldn't be measured in numbers. But in who you are as a person. Thank you for saving my planet, Raj."

It's really sweet.

I nod through the window of the sound booth to let Bob know I'm ready. It's just him and me today.

Mom was swamped with work, so she dropped me off and said she'd come get me as soon as I was done.

"We're rolling!" Bob announces. "This is line 182. Three takes in a row!"

I scroll to line 182 and lean into the microphone.

RAJ REDDY

Catch you in the galaxy, Dobrink!

"Catch you in the galaxy, Dobrink!" I say the first take full of excitement.

"Catch you in the galaxy, Dobrink." I lower my voice to just above a whisper.

"Catch you in the galaxy, Dobriiiiiiink!" I call out the third take like I'm soaring off into outer space.

Except that when I yell "Dobrink" the "ee" glides up and bounces around my voice box. I sound like a dying cat.

"Sorry about that," I say. I cough into my fist, hoping that Josh will just think I've got a frog in my throat. "Can I try that last take one more time?"

"Of course," Josh answers.

"Catch you in the gaaAAaee—" I start, but this time my voice cracks before I even get to the end of the line.

I cough even harder.

"Hey, buddy," Josh says. "Do you need some water?"

"Yes! I do! That's a great idea!"

Bob bustles into the booth and sets a bottle of water on the music stand next to me. Then he unfurls his fist and hands me a lozenge. He winks and scurries back out.

"Take your time," Josh says. "Whenever you're ready."

I roll the lozenge around my tongue, back and forth, feeling the syrupy tanginess stream into my throat. I take a sip of water. I spit the lozenge into a Kleenex and give Bob a thumbs-up.

"Rolling on line 182. Pick up, on the third take!" he says.

I lean into the microphone.

"Catch you in the galaxy, Dobrink!"

It comes out totally normal.

I wipe the sweat off my brow and head out of the booth.

Bob is hunched over his computer, downloading the audio files from our session. I linger behind his swivel chair, pretending to look at his antique radios.

"What is it, kiddo?" he asks.

"Did I . . ." I tug on the cuff of my long-sleeve shirt. "Did I sound okay in there?"

He swings around, and his chair squeaks under his weight. "Why do you ask?"

I try to smile, but I feel like if I move the muscles in my face too much, I might start to cry.

"Just 'cause . . . well, my voice," I say. "Is it . . . ?" I can't bring myself to finish the sentence.

Bob's eyebrows crinkle together. Then he leans forward in his chair and looks me straight in the eye. "Nikhil, if you want, I can play back the audio files for you. But you were terrific. Like always."

I nod, trying to believe him.

When I get home, Nana is snoring in his recliner, his legs propped up and his head tilted back so his mouth hangs open. A copy of *The Monthly Prairie Dog* lies on the side table next to him. The edges of the paper are furled upward, like it's been read.

But to my surprise, at dinner no one mentions the article. Not even Mom.

Later that night, I'm doing my homework in my room, with the door open, when from the living room I hear Nana ask, "What is this, Deepa?"

"What is what?" Mom answers.

There's a pause. Then Mom says, "Oh shoot. Nikhil's newspaper article!" She sucks her teeth. "I feel terrible. I started reading it in the morning, and then the phone started ringing nonstop! It's good, though, right? It seems like his classmates really love him."

"What does it mean, he's gay?"

"What does it—" I hear the sounds of paper rustling. A few moments go by and then she murmurs, "Oh wow. Look at that. He was so open about it in the interview. I'm so proud of him. I should go talk to him."

I hear footsteps coming my way, but Nana stops them. "What do you mean, you're proud? Why is he saying he's 'gay'?" His voice is agitated. "And why in the school newspaper? What will people think?"

"What will people think?" Mom sounds shocked. "What do you mean, what will people think?" Then her words come out slowly. Measured. "I, for one, would hope people will respect him, and admire his courage."

"Respect *this*?" Nana gets louder. "What are you teaching him?"

I slide off the bed and lean against the doorway to my room.

He keeps going. "First cartoons. Then *this*! This

is not right for our family!"

When Mom answers, there's a trembling underneath her words. "I don't want to upset you, Dad. It's not good for your health. But enough. This is who Nikhil is, and I'm proud of him. And as far as the cartoon goes . . ." Her voice gets stronger. "I don't know why you can't understand this. But Nikhil's TV show is important. Okay? It might seem silly to you, but kids look up to his character. *Indian* kids, too! Who so rarely get to see themselves on TV. Do you know how many families, just like ours, send letters to the network? Saying how much it means that their kids get to watch a character like Nikhil's? What he's doing matters!"

She waits. But Nana doesn't say anything.

Nani must come into the living room, because I hear her ask, "What happened? Is everything okay?"

Mom goes on. "I'm proud of Nikhil. And maybe, by talking about who he is so openly, he can be a role model to even *more* kids."

Nana clears his throat, and the sound echoes inside his chest. "This is not the kind of role model this family should be."

"What happened?" Nani asks again. "Amar, did you do something?"

But nobody says anything.

And then Mom's voice comes in so softly I can barely hear it. "I don't know what kind of family you think we are, but maybe this is why we haven't visited you in so many years."

I hear her footsteps coming down the hall.

I pull the door shut, carefully turning the doorknob so it won't make a noise when the latch clicks.

I throw my headphones over my ears and arrange myself cross-legged on the bed.

Mom knocks on my door, but I pretend not to hear it.

She knocks again, but I still don't answer. Finally, the door opens a crack.

I pretend to listen to my music. Mom pats me on the back, and I jump.

Worry lines form along the sides of her eyes. "Nikhil?" she asks.

"Sorry, I didn't hear you come in." I pull off my headphones and hold them out to her. "I guess I had my music on too loud."

She searches my face. "You didn't hear us talking in the living room just now? Nana and me?"

"Unh-unh." I shake my head. "Is everything okay?"

She sits next to me on the bed, covered in my new navy bedspread. We never did buy a *Minecraft* poster, but an arrangement of glow-in-the-dark planet stickers are beginning to shine on the ceiling above me. "Nikhil, are you sure you didn't hear anything?"

"Mm-hmm." I cross my fingers behind my back. "Why?"

Her lips are creased together. "No reason." Then the corners of her mouth turn up. "Listen. I just wanted to tell you . . . that I read the article in the school paper! I'm sorry I didn't get to finish it this morning! But, Nikhil, it's really great. I'm so proud of you! That took a lot of courage for you to be so open and honest about who you are." She squeezes my knee. "How are you feeling about it?"

I shrug. "All right, I guess."

"Yeah? And did it go well at school? I mean, no one caused you any trouble, did they?"

I take a breath. "Actually, everyone was really nice. In fact . . ." I chew on the inside of my cheek. "You're not going to believe this, but everyone applauded for me at lunch. It was really cool."

Mom's face glows. There's a wetness behind her eyes, and I wonder if it's because she's happy for me, or if it's because she's still upset with Nana. "Oh,

Nikhil, that's wonderful. Of course they did! You're amazing, kiddo, you know that?"

I roll my eyes. "Staaaahp," I say. And then because I don't know what else to do, I play-punch her thigh. Mom reaches her fingers out and air-tickles my stomach. I curl away, but she reaches even closer.

"Nooooo!" I scream. "I'm too old for this!"

But she doesn't tickle me. She wraps her arms around me and holds me tight.

I let Streak sleep in bed with me that night.

I curl up next to him, replaying in my head all the awful things Nana said.

Thinking about his words makes my stomach hurt, and I grab at the sheets, twisting them around in my fist.

He's your nana, I tell myself. *He loves you.*

But *does* he?

Because it's starting to feel like I can't do anything right when it comes to him.

I stare up at the stars on the ceiling, until finally, I fall asleep.

CHAPTER 19

I wake up groggy, the sheets all tangled around me. There's a pit in my stomach at the thought of having to see Nana. I tiptoe to the bathroom to shower, hoping not to run into him. Then I sit on my bed, my packed-up book bag ready to go right next to me.

But I don't move.

I don't come out for so long that finally, Nani knocks on my door.

"Nikhil, beta? Are you okay?"

I don't answer.

The doorknob turns, and Mom peeks in over Nani's head. "Hey, is everything all right?" she asks.

"We're going to be late if we don't leave soon."

"Sorry." I slide off the bed. "I'm coming."

When we get to school, Mom pulls into a parking space instead of turning into the carpool lane.

"What are you doing?" I ask, getting out of the car.

"Oh, I just have a quick meeting with Principal Dawson." She casually shuts her door and presses the Lock button on her keys.

"You do?" I eye her. "What for?"

"He just wanted to check in on a few things." She shrugs off my question. "You know, parent-teacher stuff."

"Don't they have whole days set aside for that? Like, parent-teacher conferences or something?"

I glance around the parking lot. It's emptying out. There are only two cars left in the carpool lane, and a few stray kids are jogging toward the main entrance of the school. The sky is gray, and two large rain clouds threaten to burst open above us.

I pull my jacket tighter around me. "Mom? What's going on?"

She ushers me toward the sidewalk. Her face looks strained. "I just need to talk to Principal Dawson, that's all. But I promise, I'll tell you more about it tonight. I don't want you to be late for class. We'll talk after school." Then she adds, "And don't worry, okay?"

I watch Mom duck into the main office.

Who says "don't worry" unless there's something to worry about?

All day long, I can't concentrate. Everything just feels like a blur. And as I'm turning the corner to get from science to math, I see Principal Dawson surrounded by a group of students. He's a tall Black man who always wears a crisp suit and tie. He's usually all smiles, but when he looks up at me, his concerned expression makes me nervous and I hurry away.

After school, Mom rests her hand on my knee the whole drive home. I follow her down to the basement, and she pulls up a chair for me at her desk.

"Nikhil, I wanted to talk to you this morning. I did. But . . . well, I needed to talk to Principal Dawson first."

I pick at my jeans, right above my knee. "About what?"

"First of all, did anything happen at school today?

Did anyone say anything . . . unusual to you?"

"No. I don't think so."

"Good." She nods. "Listen, I'm pretty sure this will all blow over. But I want you to know what's going on, just in case anyone tries to stir up any trouble. I'd rather you hear it from me first than find out some other way."

I grip the seat of my chair.

"And I want you to know that I'm really proud of you. For being who you are. And for talking about it so openly in the school paper. This doesn't change any of that. If anything, it makes me even more proud. Okay?"

My chest feels like it's going to close in on itself.

"So, last night, after you went to bed, Principal Dawson reached out to me." Mom starts slowly. "He got a call from a woman whose daughter used to go to Sycamore." I see a flash of anger behind her eyes. "She's not even a parent here anymore. So it's none of her business! But—" Mom takes a deep breath. "Well, you know the word 'homophobic,' right?" She looks at me. "We've talked about what that means?"

I nod. My fists are balled up tight against my legs.

"Well, she's homophobic. That's what she is. And it turns out this woman still reads the school paper online—even though, *again*, it's none of her business! But it upset her . . ." This time when Mom inhales, her shoulders rise up an inch. "Well, it upset her that you talked about being gay in the paper. So, she's trying to cause problems."

I squeeze my eyebrows together. My mind drifts to Nana.

Mom leans forward. "Nikhil, I don't want you to worry. Principal Dawson assured me he will not tolerate any kind of hurtful or hateful behavior. He's incredibly supportive. The whole school is! In fact, he said that yesterday in the teachers' lounge, all the teachers were singing your praises!" Mom pauses, watching my face. "And listen, I asked for this woman's information so I could talk to her. But Principal Dawson thinks it's best to just leave everything alone for now. But I promise you. If she tries *anything* . . ." Mom trails off, and now her eyes look furious.

We both sit there for a minute. Then I ask, "What do you mean if she tries anything? What would she try?" My voice comes out smaller than I expect it to.

Mom shakes her head. "I'm sorry. I made that

sound scarier than I needed to. I honestly don't think she'll try anything. At all. In my experience, people like her are mostly just looking for attention." She takes my hand in hers and rubs her thumb across the top of mine. She exhales. "Oh, Nikhil. I wish I could shield you from these things. Forever." She rests her palm against my cheek. "But you need to know that, even though you should *always* be proud of who you are . . . sometimes, there will be people who try to make you feel bad about the very things that make you special. And I can't always hide that from you, as much as I wish I could."

I feel a pressure building up inside me. I have a feeling that Mom's not telling me everything. "Right, but, if she did try something, what would it be?"

Mom holds my hand a little tighter.

"Well . . ." Then she says, delicately, "I don't know. But what she told Principal Dawson is"—she hesitates—"well, that she doesn't want you to be the lead of the musical." Mom sounds exasperated. "Which is ridiculous!"

"Why would she care about that?" I ask.

"That's a very good question!" Mom furrows her brow. "See, Nikhil, she thinks that because you're on

TV, the other kids look up to you. Which is true. And that's a good thing! But because she's homophobic, she doesn't like that. And so, she's decided that, if she can just keep you off that stage, maybe the kids will look up to you a little less." She lifts her chin. "It doesn't make any sense, because people like her don't tend to think logically. They're just grasping at straws. Trying to find anything to make them feel like they've won."

She leans in. "But you need to hear this, okay? Principal Dawson, myself, the other teachers, and— from what you told me—the rest of the students, we all *love* you and we can't wait for you to be up on that stage! And even more so now!"

I try to nod, but I can't seem to get my head to move the way I want it to. "Okay."

Mom pulls me in for a hug. "And I don't want you to worry. There's no way I'm letting this woman do *anything* to hurt you! And I want you to know that you can always come talk to me. About anything."

I bury my face in Mom's shirt.

There are so many things I wish I could tell her right now.

I wish I could tell her that I don't even want to do the musical. I wish I could tell her that I overheard her and Nana. I wish I could tell her that I'm scared about what's happening to my voice.

But for some reason, I don't.

CHAPTER 20

The next couple weeks, I feel like I'm looking over my shoulder all the time. Like some angry mom is going to suddenly pop up behind my locker door. Or come storming into the middle of algebra and scream at me in front of the entire class.

But, luckily, that doesn't happen.

At home, I avoid Nana as much as I can. I try to keep our dinner conversations focused only on school-work. I amaze myself at how excited I can sound about things I have no interest in, like the Pythagorean theorem.

After school, we only have one more musical rehearsal. I guess Mrs. Reed meant it when she said things wouldn't pick up until after the winter. And thankfully, I don't have to sing. Instead, she hands out the rest of the solos.

"Doing double duty as both Evan in *Dear Evan Hansen* and Kristoff in *Frozen*, let's give it up for"—she twirls her arm in the air and bows with a flourish—"our very own De-See-aaaan!"

DeSean leaps to his feet to grab his sheet music, puffing his chest out as wide as Kristoff's. "Your hair, my princess! It's turning white!" he says in an over-the-top Kristoff voice, and even though it's totally hammy, we all giggle.

"And who better to play our mischievous child genius, Matilda in *Matilda*, than—" Mrs. Reed holds her breath so long that the rest of us scream out, "Monicaaaaa!"

Monica pumps both her fists.

Mateo and I are so happy for both her and DeSean, whooping out loud, that for a minute I forget all about the tension between us, and what's happening with my voice, and the woman who called Principal Dawson.

Things even start going better at the studio. Bob offers me a cup of hot water and a packet of honey before my recording sessions, which I eagerly gulp down. But for the most part, I don't even need it. My voice seems to be behaving itself. At least for now.

And then, a few weeks later, Anton's coming to visit!

"Please fasten your seatbelts and switch your electronic devices to Airplane Mode. We are just about ready for takeoff!" The sound of a flight attendant's voice interrupts my video call with him.

The dark blue sleeve of his puffy coat fills the screen of his phone. When his face pops back in, he's holding a vomit bag.

"I seriously might throw up!" He waves the bag at me. "We're really going to Wright-Patterson Air Force Base?"

I laugh. "Yes! Okay, you need to hang up. Your plane's about to take off! I'll see you in a few hours!"

His phone slips out of his hand, and I catch a glimpse of the woman sitting next to him. She doesn't look pleased. "You really need to turn that phone off, kid. And if you're planning to vomit, do you think maybe you'd like the aisle seat?"

I see Anton's fingers clutch the armrest. "I'd

prefer the window. I'm hoping to get an aerial view of a crop circle."

He picks his phone back up and flips it around. "Nikhil." He swallows. "Okay. You're right. I've gotta go. But—"

Two long fingers with nail polish hover over the phone. Then the call ends.

I make Mom drive us to the airport early. Since Anton's traveling alone, she has to go to the gate to pick him up. So, Nani and I wait on the sidewalk outside the baggage claim. The air is cold, but the sun beats down on our faces, and when my phone vibrates with the text message, I'm heeeeeeere! I actually start dancing, right there in front of everyone. Even Nani joins in!

Minutes later, Anton's entire body is pressed up against the glass window of the automatic revolving door. His puffy coat hangs open, and his duffel bag is slung across his chest. Just behind the strap, I see his NASA T-shirt.

"That flight was phenomenal!" he says. Then he digs into his coat pocket and pulls out four mini bags of pretzels. "The woman next to me fell asleep just as the snacks were coming out, so the flight attendant said I could have extra!"

We Vulcan salute. Then I throw my arms around him.

The next morning, Anton and I toss our R2-D2 and C-3PO shirts on over our jeans. In the end, I asked DeSean, Monica, and Mateo about their trick-or-treating plans. But even though we talked about maybe meeting up, things are still kind of strained between us. And I'm not sure if Anton really wants to hang out with them anyhow. In any case, at least we'll already be half-dressed this way if we do decide to get together.

We pile into the back seat of Mom's Subaru.

"Coming in for a landing at Wright-Patterson!" Mom uses her intercom voice as she drives just past the base. "Agents, please be on high alert for any extraterrestrial sightings!"

Anton and I stare out the window, and our jaws drop.

Wright-Patterson is one of the largest air force bases in the entire country. Massive airplane hangars sprawl out behind rows of military flags, and off in the distance enormous jetliners are lined up on the tarmac, their noses gleaming in the sun.

Mom pulls into a parking space at the museum—which is just down the street from the actual base—and we all head in. While she has her purse scanned at the X-ray machine, Anton and I dart over to the display case filled with maps for all the exhibits.

He runs his fingers along the pamphlets. "Do you think they have a map that shows Hangar Eighteen?"

Last night, we'd read all the articles we could find on the internet about Wright-Patterson. The story—according to a lot of very credible websites—is that in 1947, the US government hid pieces of a crashed UFO and the bodies of several three-foot-tall aliens right here, in the basement of Hangar Eighteen.

Which is *not* part of the museum tour.

"Ready?" Mom catches up to us. "What do you want to see first?"

We walk through rooms filled with all kinds of aircraft. There are wooden planes with wheels that look like bicycle tires and fighter jets with stars on their wings. There's even a plane with the face of a shark painted across the front.

The whole time we're walking, Anton has one eye on the map in his hands.

When Mom stops for a restroom break, we wait near the vending machines for her.

"I found it! It's just past there!" he whispers excitedly. Then he points down the hall at a glass door marked "Personnel Only—No Visitors Allowed."

He unfurls the map, and my eyes follow his finger as he traces a path from where we're standing, just past the door, and then across a large green lawn that leads back to the base. His fingertip lands on Hangar Eighteen.

"It's so far away." I try to keep my voice down. "And, besides, that door is off-limits! What should we do?"

"I don't know!" His entire forehead is scrunched up. "You think your mom would have any ideas?"

"Do I—? Are you kidding? You really think my mom's going to help us break into an area that's closed to visitors?"

Anton looks disappointedly at the map. "Well, should we at least go look through the door? See if there's another possibility?"

"It's off-limits!"

But now I feel like I might pee my pants, just thinking about how close we are to the bodies of actual aliens.

"I guess it doesn't hurt to look," I say. We both start walking, fast, toward the door. We must be going too fast, because I don't even know how it happens, but somehow I crash into Anton and his body slams right against the door handle.

The door doesn't budge.

Instead, a deafening alarm goes off.

We immediately cover our ears. Everyone around us does, too.

It all happens so fast that by the time Mom's coming out of the bathroom, the alarm has been silenced, and Anton and I are surrounded by two security guards.

"What on earth?" Mom wipes her hands along the front of her pants. "I was gone for two minutes! What did you kids do?"

"Sorry," we mumble.

"It's all right, ma'am," one of the guards says. "This isn't the first time we've had alien-crazy kids stirring up trouble. But I am going to have to ask the three of you to cut your visit here short today. It's kind of museum policy."

"Of course," Mom sighs. "I truly apologize." She flashes a look of disappointment at Anton and me. "Boys. Anything you want to say to the nice guards?"

"Sorry," we mumble again.

The other guard tips her hat at us. Then she says, "Well, we gotta skedaddle. It's"—she clutches her stomach—"it's alien feeding time at Hangar Eighteen!"

Anton and I hang our heads as she lets out a huge belly laugh.

We ride silently in the back seat of Mom's car most of the way home. But when she drives past the exit we normally take to get to Nana and Nani's house and keeps heading down the highway, I look up at her in the rearview mirror.

"I seem to remember," she says, "this place where you might be able to find some aliens. If memory serves me right"—she lowers her voice—"it's a corn-field where a UFO once landed. Should we try to find it?"

A smile peeks out across Anton's face. "You'd really take us there, after all that?"

I'm not sure if Mom's just being nice because that's who she is, or if it's because she knows how much Anton and I have been looking forward to today.

Whatever the reason, I mouth, "Thanks, Mom."

Minutes later, we're pulling up a dusty driveway to a place called Bramblewoods Farms. A man in

165

a headless scarecrow costume greets us inside the wooden gates. "Careful not to lose your head in here, like I did!" he says in a spooky voice.

It's groan-worthy, but Anton and I mumble back, "We'll try not to!"

"I'll go get the tickets for the corn maze!" Mom says. "That's"—she waves her fingers in our faces—"where the UFO landed."

A few minutes later, she's jogging back over to us.

"Since we got here so late, they only have tickets left for the last time of the day. Is that all right?" she asks, checking her watch. "It'll make us too late to join the rest of your friends for trick-or-treating. If you still wanted to do that."

I look at Anton, trying to read his expression.

"I'm okay with whatever." I shrug.

A wave of what looks like relief crosses his face. Then he tilts his chin up at Mom. To my surprise, he says, "Honestly, Ms. Shah, we're getting a little old for trick-or-treating anyway."

We spend the afternoon dunking apples in hot caramel sauce, and pushing each other in a tire swing so high that our stomachs feel like they're going to leap out of our mouths. Then, just before the sun starts to dip over the edge of the horizon, we catch the last hayride to the corn maze.

The maze stretches out so far, you can't see the end of it.

Mom holds up a pair of tickets. "I thought it'd be nice for you boys to have your *own* adventure. Just the two of you. So, I only bought two tickets." She glances at the sky that's already turning a deep blue. "But stay close to the others and keep your phones on. Don't set off any alarms! And come back before it's too late, okay?" Then she winks. "And if you see any aliens, don't forget to take a selfie!"

We load up the app for the maze on my phone, and Anton and I head down the dirt path, under a sign that reads, *Enter at Your Own Risk.*

"Should we walk along the outer perimeter?" he asks.

Our footsteps crunch against the fallen stalks of corn strewn across the mud. Even though this maze is clearly man-made, it's easy to imagine that maybe, just maybe, a UFO landed here.

Last night was a whirlwind when Anton arrived. But, we haven't been alone like this in months—just quiet—and while we're both keeping our eyes peeled for aliens, I realize how much there is to catch up on.

"Hey," I ask, under my breath, as if talking too

loudly might scare off any hidden creatures. "How's stuff in LA?"

"Good, good." He rubs his hands together, blowing on them to keep them warm.

"Yeah? I forgot to ask. But. Whatever happened with that whole birthday party thing? With Melissa?"

"Umm . . . Believe it or not, I went!"

"Wait. You did? How was it?"

"It was actually a lot of fun!" he says, almost too enthusiastically.

"Nice!" I smile. "That's awesome!"

"Yup!" He reaches his hand out and punches one of the cornstalks. "And"—he shrugs—"I made sure my shoelaces were double-knotted this time!"

I let out a chuckle.

We keep walking, the corn swaying over our heads.

"How's the musical going?" he asks.

"Good," I say. And then, I double down. "It's actually going really well!"

"See?" He smiles. "I knew you should do it!"

"Mm-hmm." I nod.

We take a few more steps.

And then—I don't know if it's because of the adrenaline of the day, or if it's because I've had all this pressure bottling up inside me, or if it's because I'm finally hanging out with my best friend in the whole world and I don't want to lie to him—but everything comes tumbling out of me. "Honestly, it's not going well at all!" I sigh. "I mean, it's messing up everything with all my new friends here. And I think it's pretty obvious to *everyone* that I'm a terrible singer!" My words start to come out sharper. Faster. Like I'm losing control of them. "I got interviewed in the school paper about it, and I told the kid who was interviewing me that I was gay. Which is cool. But it's not *just* the school that found out. My grandfather read the article! And Anton, you wouldn't believe what he said about it. He said all these *really* awful . . ." I shake my head. "And then this woman called the principal, and she's even worse than my grandfather . . . She's . . ." I try to catch my breath. "Oh. And another thing—"

I stop myself, just as I'm about to tell Anton that my voice is cracking.

For some reason, I feel like if I say it out loud, it'll be too real, and I'll never be able to shove it back down and lock it away.

Now that my rant's over, I realize how quiet it

is. We must have wandered away from the rest of the parkgoers, because I don't hear any other people around us.

I hang my head. "I wish we'd never moved here in the first place! I miss you, Anton!"

My voice echoes against the stalks of corn, and a breeze ruffles through the maze.

There's an earthy smell coming from the ground.

Then Anton stops walking, and I hear him mutter under his breath, "Melissa's party was terrible."

"What?" I ask.

"I only talked to her for, like, a minute." His head is facing down. "Everyone else there was . . . Well, it was all the same kids. You know. The ones who act like I don't even exist. I. . ." He closes his eyes, and now I'm pretty sure I hear his voice catch. "I made my mom come pick me up early."

We're stopped in the middle of the maze now.

"I didn't know things were so bad here," he says. "I'm sorry. In my mind . . ." A muscle ripples along his jaw. "Well, I thought you'd made all these new friends . . . and that . . ."

"That what?"

"That . . ." He looks off to the side. "I don't know . . ."

"What, Anton?"

Then, even though I'm pretty sure he's trying to tell me that he's afraid I'm moving on from him, he catches me off guard. "I mean, what do they say?" he asks. "Your friends here? Have you tried talking to any of them about all this?"

My lips part. I'm not sure how to answer him.

The truth is, I haven't.

Everyone here's been doing their best to be supportive. It's me who's been avoiding talking about, well, lots of things.

"Maybe I should," I say.

I put my hand on his shoulder. "I'm really sorry about Melissa's party," I tell him. "But it's cool you gave it a shot."

Around us the sky is growing pitch-black, and I realize how late it must be. "What time is it, anyway?" I ask. "We probably need to head back."

I peer at my phone. But the app seems stuck, so I swipe down, trying to refresh it.

Only, the strangest thing happens. The screen of my phone flashes bright white three times, like a flickering lightbulb, and then it goes completely dark.

"Shoot!" I shake it. "What happened?" Without

the light from the phone, it's impossible to see more than a foot in front of us.

"Did the battery die?" Anton asks.

"I charged it all last night!" I shake my head.

"Did you lose service?"

"I don't know." I hold it up in the air, trying to catch a signal. The tips of the cornstalks tower over us, their edges bathed in moonlight.

"Hello?" I call out. But no one answers.

And then Anton's hand shoots straight up, pointing at the sky.

"Nikhil, look!"

Way up over our heads, something is glowing bright white. It's way too big to be a star or a plane.

It's round. And it hovers in the sky like a . . . Could it be a . . . ?

There's no way!

Our jaws hang open. I will my feet to move, but they won't.

Then suddenly, the cornstalks next to us start to shake violently. Something glows inside them that looks like tiny little pairs of red eyes.

"AAAAAAAAAAAAAAAHHHHHHHHH!!!!!!"
We scream in each other's faces and tear down the

path, instinctively choosing which way to go.

I want to tell myself that there's a perfectly reasonable explanation for what we saw.

That it was just a plane in the sky. And someone playing a prank in the cornstalks.

All I know is that Anton and I scream our heads off the entire way back, and that somehow our feet find the entrance to the maze just in time to meet Mom for the last hayride out of Bramblewoods.

Later that night, Anton and I lie tucked inside sleeping bags on the floor of my room. We stare at the stickers glowing on my ceiling.

There's not a sound in the entire house.

"Hey, Anton," I whisper. "This was the best weekend ever."

But when I turn to look at him, he's already snoring.

CHAPTER 21

I want to open up to my friends. To muster up the courage to do exactly what Anton said. But it's harder than I thought. I'm not even sure where to start.

And then, at lunch one day, Monica pulls a printed-out email from her backpack and lays it on our table. The four of us have to scoot in closer together to read it.

"I overheard my mom and dad talking about this last night," she tells us. "They were reading it on my mom's computer. After dinner, my mom left her laptop open, and I printed it out while she wasn't looking." She lays a hand on my arm. "I'm really sorry, Nikhil."

With every word I read, it gets harder to breathe. I'm mad. I'm really mad.

But it's not just me who's upset. I can tell by the way Mateo's jaw is set that he's fighting back tears. And a vein is popping out along the side of DeSean's neck.

From: Constance Shaffer

To: Undisclosed recipients

Subject: We must protect our children

Dear Sycamore Parents,

It's come to my attention that a new student started Sycamore Middle this year. Nikhil Shah is an 8th grader who also happens to be an openly homosexual TV star. Many of our youngsters watch the cartoon he stars in on a regular basis. Now, he's flaunting his homosexuality in the school newspaper.

Which means our precious middle schoolers—who should not even be thinking about sex yet—are being told "it's great to be gay" by someone they look up to!

It makes me sick just to think about it, and I'm sure you feel the same way.

To make matters worse, Nikhil is playing the lead in the school musical—just one more reason for our kids to look up to him. I called Principal Dawson to demand that the school remove him from this role, but he refused to listen. So, the time has come to take matters into our own hands.

Nikhil Shah and his LGBT agenda have no place in our school!

If Principal Dawson won't do anything about it, it's up to us to stop this from happening!

If you believe in saving our kids, please email me your interest ASAP.

Yours,

Constance Shaffer

"Is this"—my voice quivers—"for *real*?" I know this woman called the school, but something about seeing all these words makes my stomach turn all over again. And if Monica's mom got this, does that mean everyone's parents did?

I glance around the cafeteria.

But at all the other tables, kids just seem to be eating their lunches like they normally do.

"Do you know who else got this?" I ask. "Did she send it to the whole school?"

Monica shakes her head. "I don't know! I heard my mom say she doesn't even know how this woman has her info. She thought maybe it was from an old PTA list or something?"

I turn to DeSean. "Did your moms get it?" Panic is rising in my chest.

He grits his teeth. "If they had, I'm pretty sure I would have heard something."

I stare at the paper until the words start swimming across the page.

They make me feel . . . what *is* that? Shame?

Mateo's head is buried in his hands. I wish I could tell him that this isn't our fault.

But then, why do I feel so bad?

The bell rings, and before we head to class, I ask Monica if I can keep the printout.

That night, I knock on Mom's door. For some reason, I'm so nervous to show her the email that my hand trembles.

Her eyes race back and forth as she reads it. Her fingers clutch the paper until the edges crumple in her hands.

"She can't actually do anything to me, can she?" I ask.

"No. No, Nikhil. She can't." Mom holds me. "I'm going to put an end to this whole thing right now!"

I'm sitting on my floor when I hear Mom's raised voice on the phone coming from inside her bedroom. Her anger courses down the hall. It makes Streak whimper. I know Mom's talking to Principal Dawson because I hear her say things like, "Well, is there anything else I can do? I will go to the school board! Or the district! Or the county! Or wherever I have to go! But I am not letting her threaten my son!"

A few minutes later, I hear what sounds like knocking on Mom's door, and then Nana's voice asks, "Why are you yelling? What is it?"

"It's this!" Mom says. "Read it!" There's a long pause, and then Mom says, "You say you want the best for your grandson. But you're no different than this woman. If you really care about Nikhil, then ask yourself, have you *once* tried to listen to him? To understand him? Have you ever tried to understand *anyone* in this family? Or do you only care about yourself?"

I wrap my hands around the back of my head. I'm expecting Nana to say that this is exactly what he was worried about. That this woman is going to ruin our family's reputation.

Instead, there's a confusion in his voice when he says, "But, who is she?"

"I don't know!" Mom practically yells.

I lift my head up.

After a long silence, I hear the sound of Mom's door being slammed.

The next day at school, Principal Dawson brings the entire student body together for a special assembly. He doesn't mention the email, and he doesn't mention me by name. But by the way everyone is fidgeting in the gymnasium bleachers, I'm pretty sure that by now, they all know exactly what this is about. "I want to assure each of you, no matter how you identify, or who you are, hate has no place here," he says. "This school is a safe space, and we will always protect you."

A few kids nod knowingly in my direction, a look of solidarity in their eyes. And from three rows down, Kyle turns toward me and mouths, "I'm sorry." I shake my head to let him know this isn't his fault.

As we all file out, Mrs. Reed squeezes my shoulder. But, honestly, I just don't want any more attention.

CHAPTER 22

"**L**et's just grab one more take!" Josh says. Even though he's two thousand miles away, I'm pretty sure I can hear the sound of his disappointment in my headphones. "The acting on that read was spot-on, it's just . . . can you pitch it up a *smidge* higher?"

I unwrap a lozenge and stick it in my mouth. I take a sip of hot water to clear my throat. Bob nods at me encouragingly through the window of the sound booth.

My voice isn't cracking today. But I can't get it to sound as high as it normally does. I lean into the microphone. I'm about to try again when Josh says,

"Actually, hang on one second! We're going to fiddle around with that last take and see if we can salvage it on our end. The acting was so good!"

My headphones go pin-drop silent. I can't hear Josh in Los Angeles. And I can't hear Bob. The only sound is my own breath, going in and out.

"We're all set over here!" Josh's voice flies back in. "Just took a little tweak with the engineering! Nice work, Nikhil! That's a wrap!"

"Are you sure?" I suck on my lip. "I'm really sorry. I think my voice is just tired. Plus, it's getting really cold here!" I say. "It's winter! Maybe I'm coming down with something?"

"No need to be sorry. Listen, buddy, we're going to be shutting down for a few weeks with the holidays coming up anyhow. So just take it easy and rest up, okay?"

"Okay." I search Josh's words for any hint of concern.

"And, oh!" he says excitedly. "I'm going to email your mom about this, but Cartoon Con is coming up in a few months! We want to fly you to LA for it. We'll be doing a live table read of the season finale script of *RROS*, in front of hundreds of fans! It's gonna be awesome. What do you think?"

Reading a script, *live*, in front of hundreds of people?

I swallow.

Cartoon Con is one of the biggest animation events of the year. All the big shows are there. Do I really have a choice?

Then again, maybe it'd be fun.

Plus, if Josh wants to fly me out to LA for this, maybe he *hasn't* noticed anything.

I take another sip of water. Then I grin and squeeze out my best Raj Reddy voice. "Cartoon Con, here I come!"

The sound of Josh's laughter fills my headphones.

CHAPTER 23

Winter break brings snow. A lot of it. It comes down hard and fast, covering the ground in blankets of white.

I've seen snow before, but never like this. Never in my own backyard. There's so much of it that it looks like we live inside a snow globe.

As I stare at all the snowflakes, flurrying down outside my window, I can feel the stress of the last few weeks melting away, and after breakfast, I take a chance and group-message Mateo, DeSean, and Monica.

Hey. Would you all be up for a snowball fight?

At my place? ⛄

I wait with bated breath for their responses. Monica's comes in first, followed quickly by Mateo.

Monica: I'm in!

Mateo: Suh-weeet! ❄

And I finally exhale when DeSean writes:

DeSean: Sounds like fun!

When everyone gets here, Nani pulls a wool hat down over my ears and ushers the four of us into the backyard. Streak nips at our heels as we dart down the patio stairs. We all fall knee-deep into the piles of fluff, and things feel normal between us again.

We're making snow angels, fanning our arms and legs in and out, when I sit up and catch Nana watching us. He's seated in a chair by his bedroom window, and—even though the heat is blasting in the house—he's wearing a thick, knit sweater and a dark gray winter hat just like mine.

I keep my head down, so he won't know I'm looking. But out of the corner of my eye, I see Mom come in behind him. She puts something in the palm of his hand. It must be his pills, because she offers him a glass of water. As he swallows them down, I see her patting his back.

"Are we having this snowball fight or what?" Monica pops up. She kicks up the snow with her hand, making little flakes dance all around her. "Let's call teams!"

As soon as she says "teams," Mateo glances in my direction. One of his eyebrows is arched. But the thought of being alone with him makes my stomach so squirrely that before I can stop myself, I blurt out, "I call DeSean!"

We head to opposite ends of the yard to build forts, piling snow into walls as high as our waists. DeSean and I are huddled behind ours, packing together an arsenal of snowballs, when I work up the courage to say, "Hey, DeSean? I've been wanting to tell you that . . ." I force the words out. "Well. I'm sorry."

He cocks his head. "What do you mean?"

"I mean." I take a breath. "About the musical. I

just feel like ever since I got cast as the lead, things have gotten so weird. And I . . . well, I wish they weren't." My voice grows quieter. Then I ask, "Are you mad at me?"

DeSean runs his mittened hand across his forehead. "I'm not . . ." His lips part, like he's searching for the words. "I'm not sure how I feel, okay? Maybe I am a little mad. I don't know. But not at *you*. It's not your fault. I guess . . . well, you're right, it's been kind of weird. And I don't want it to be either. You're my friend! But . . . I thought. I mean Mrs. Reed *told* me—"

Monica calls from across the yard, "You guys almost ready?"

"Just a few more minutes!" I shout. I turn back to him. "I know what Mrs. Reed told you. And you should one hundred percent be the lead! Everyone knows that! I only auditioned in the first place because I wanted to hang out with all of you. Because I wanted to be friends with you. But I had no idea it would turn out like this!" I try to keep the words from rushing out too fast. "To tell you the truth, I wish I could just drop out, and then you could play the part like you should have all along! But now I feel like everyone's expecting me to be up on that stage. And . . ." I pause. "I mean, everyone in our cast knows that I can't sing! At all. And my voice . . ." I scrunch up my face. I hear Anton inside my head: *Have you tried talking to your friends here?*

But I can't bring myself to do it. I can't tell DeSean that my voice is changing, any more than I can tell Anton. I don't even know why I'm so afraid to let go of Raj Reddy. But I am.

So, instead, I say, "I'm just going to drop out, okay? I'll . . . I'll call Mrs. Reed tomorrow."

"Now?" Mateo's voice bounces off the side of the oak tree.

"Another minute!" DeSean leans back against the fort. "Don't do that, Nikhil." He pauses. "I don't want you to do that. Listen, I *wanted* to be the lead. I really did. But I don't want you to drop out! Not *now*! You *can't*!" There's an anger in his voice. "You know I have two moms, right? I love them more than anything in the whole world. And if you drop out of the musical, it'll be like . . ." He trails off, and I see his eyes fill up. "Well, it'll be like that woman who wrote that email won." I can hear him fighting back the tears.

We both sit there. Trying to collect our thoughts. Trying to figure out what more to say.

"What are you guys doing over there?" Monica calls.

I know that there's so much left to talk about, but Monica and Mateo are waiting. So I swallow and say, "We probably need to go play this snowball fight, huh?"

And then, maybe because we have no other choice, DeSean nods. I see the faintest hint of a dimple forming on the side of his cheek.

"Well, if we're going to play, we might as well try to win. Right?" he says. I grin back in response.

For the next hour, we pummel each other with snowballs. Streak darts back and forth between us, barking at the top of his lungs, the reflective strips on his winter coat glowing in the fading sun.

And before I know it, we're all laughing our heads off.

Maybe it's because I finally said something to DeSean. Or who knows why. But, I feel something start to open up inside me.

Mateo throws a shot that smacks me right in the chest, and just as I'm hamming it up, clutching the front of my snowsuit and tumbling to the ground, I see Nana, still watching us from his bedroom window.

I wave at him, and to my surprise, he waves back.

CHAPTER 24

"Moana, *Luca, Coco*?" Mom scrolls through the thumbnails of streaming animated films on the television. "*Klaus*?"

It's late, but Mom, Nani, and I are wide awake, huddled under a pile of blankets on the sofa in the basement. After all the energy of our snowball fight, I just wasn't ready to let the day end. So, I convinced them we should have movie night. We're watching in the basement so we don't wake up Nana with the noise.

Streak is tuckered out, his nose buried in the crook of Nani's elbow.

"*Klaus*?" I suggest. "'Cause it's the holidays?"

Streak's head pops up, and there's a creaking noise on the basement stairs. The three of us turn. It's Nana, slowly trying to make his way down. Mom rushes over to the staircase, the muscles in her neck straining. "Dad! What are you doing? Let me help you!"

Even though Nana tries to wave her off, he grips Mom's shoulder for support. He hovers one foot over each stair, like he's afraid he won't land properly. When he gets to the bottom step, he looks up at us and grumbles, "Can I join you?"

Mom casts a surprised look at Nani, who gently nods, and we all scoot over to make room for him on the sofa.

The TV glows as the movie starts. I pull the blanket up to my shoulders.

Minutes later, Mom, Nani, and Nana have all fallen asleep. An orchestra of snores gurgles up around me—it's like they're snoring in harmony! I slide the remote out of Mom's hands and turn up the volume. The blanket shifts over my legs, and Nana's eyelids slowly part open.

He stares at the TV for a minute, and then he

turns to me, his voice thick with sleep. "Is there any movie like this, but with an Indian boy? As the main part?"

I try to think of all the animated films I've ever watched. "I'm not sure. Not that I can think of."

"Hm." He watches a little longer, and then just before he drifts back to sleep, I hear him mumble, "Maybe there should be."

The credits for the film are rolling up the screen when I hear the dinging of a text message on my phone. I slide out from under the covers, trying not to disturb anybody. Then, I tiptoe to Mom's desk.

It's DeSean.

Hey. Want to come over tomorrow? We could talk more?

I'm about to respond when he adds:

And maybe bring your sheet music?

Then one last message pops up.

We could hang out for a bit, and then I could invite Monica and Mateo to come over, too. I mean, if you want.

I'm not sure why DeSean wants me to bring my sheet music. But I know that I want to finish our conversation. I write back:

That sounds great.

CHAPTER 25

I shove my feet into a pair of snow boots, and Nani wraps my scarf so high around my face that I can barely see. Then I head down the icy sidewalk to DeSean's house, my sheet music in my backpack.

One of his moms answers the front door.

She's tall, with dark brown locs that hang to her chin. Her skin's the same color as DeSean's, and her hazel eyes match his. "You must be Nikhil! Get in here, out of the cold!" She helps me unravel my scarf, brushing away the few flakes of snow hanging from it. "I'm Tonya, DeSean's momma." She rubs her hands together and presses them against my cheeks, warming me up.

Behind her, another woman steps into the foyer. She wipes cooking flour off her hands onto a messy apron tied around her waist. She's white, with curly brown hair piled on top of her head. She wears a pair of glasses flecked with the same cooking flour that's on her fingers. "I'm Kristy, DeSean's mom!" Her eyes crinkle into a smile behind her glasses. Then she adds, "I'd give you a hug, but I'm a mess! We've been baking this morning! Pies! In fact, I was just teaching DeSean how to make a spinach-feta pie."

"Hi." I smile back and yank off my snow boots so I don't leave puddles on their floor.

Tonya and Kristy glance at one another, and then Tonya brushes her locs back behind her ear. "Nikhil, we know what's happening at the school. With that woman and her, well, horrible email. And we just wanted to tell you how brave we think you are."

For some reason, when she says it, I don't feel that same anxiety. The one that makes me wish everyone would just stop talking about me.

"When we were in middle school"—Kristy smooths the front of her apron—"we didn't know anyone who was openly gay. None of the other kids. None of our teachers."

Tonya nods. "And we certainly didn't have school

assemblies to let us know that kids like us were safe."

"I think we both just want you to know"—Kristy takes a step closer to Tonya—"that we admire your courage. And we're here for you. Don't let that woman make you doubt yourself, okay?"

"What are they saying to you?" DeSean flies in behind them. He sucks a piece of spinach off his finger. "Are they being embarrassing? Are they asking you a million questions about *RROS*?"

"Now, why on earth would we do that?" Kristy playfully snaps her apron in his direction. She turns back to me. "Although I do have a few questions!"

Tonya leans in and whispers conspiratorially, "Are Commander Marks and Captain Lykes ever going to get together? I mean, there's definitely a romance happening there, right?"

For some reason—again—I don't feel embarrassed.

But before I can answer, DeSean grabs my arm and pulls me down the hall. "And on that note, bye, Mom! Bye, Momma! The pie's in the oven!"

Posters of Broadway shows cover the walls of DeSean's bedroom, and a bunch of old theater programs are stacked on top of his desk right next to some photo frames. There's a baby picture of him, one of him taking a bow on stage, and one of him and his moms at what looks like a march. They're all wearing black T-shirts with rainbow-colored fists on the front.

Plugged in next to his closet is an electric keyboard, resting on a metal folding stand. A mud-caked football is stashed underneath it, and a bright red Ohio State Buckeyes sweatshirt lies across the keys, covering up a few pages of sheet music.

He flings himself backward on his bed and rolls his eyes. "Please tell me they didn't say anything embarrassing!"

"Not at all!" I laugh. "They're really nice!"

I sit down next to him. Then I hesitate before asking. "Do they . . ." I feel an uncomfortable pit in my stomach. "Do your moms think you should be playing the Narrator?"

DeSean sits a litte more upright. He chews his lip. "I think they were surprised. They asked if I wanted them to call Mrs. Reed to talk about it. But I didn't want them to."

I glance at the posters on his wall, not sure what more to say. "You really love being on stage, huh?"

His face lights up. "It's . . ." He takes a breath. "It's like the best feeling in the world."

He eyes the backpack that I've dropped by my feet. "Speaking of, did you bring your sheet music?" He hops off the bed and tosses his sweatshirt on the floor. He nudges the football underneath the keyboard with his toe and shoves it away from the pedal. Then he flicks on the power switch. "Yesterday, when we were talking . . . well, I know that you're really worried about the singing. So, I thought. Well, if you want . . . I could help you with some of it."

"Really?" I ask. "But wouldn't that be weird for you?"

"Listen, Nikhil. The show is cast the way it's cast. And I'm happy for you. Seriously." He runs his fingers along the edge of his keyboard. "Besides, I know how Broadway works! There'll probably be a million parts that I audition for that I don't get. He turns back to face me. "And I already told you. I don't want you to drop out! Not for me. And not . . . because of that woman!"

I swallow. "Okay." I reach for my bag and pull out my music, then hand it to DeSean.

As he fiddles around on his keyboard, teaching himself how to play the music, he lightly sings the songs himself.

Once he's figured out the opening number, he

asks me to come join him.

But I hold back. What if he hears something glitch in my voice?

DeSean's beckoning me, and I'm trying to work up the courage to go over there when the door to his room flies open.

It's Mateo. His curls are matted down from his mustard-colored winter hat, which he holds in his hands. And his cheeks are flushed from the cold. Monica's right behind him, her fuzzy white turtleneck pulled all the way up to her chin.

My eyes go wide.

DeSean must see the panic on my face, because he asks, "Wait. You guys are here already?"

"Mm-hmm." Monica closes the door behind her. "Isn't this when you asked us to come?"

DeSean glances at the alarm clock on his desk. "Oh. Right. I guess I should've given us more time."

"For what?" Mateo asks.

Monica eyes the sheet music on DeSean's keyboard. "What are you guys doing?"

DeSean turns to me, a questioning look in his eyes.

"Nothing!" I say, quickly.

Mateo's eyes dart back and forth between us.

"DeSean was just going to help me with some of my songs, okay?" I try to sound as casual as possible. "For the musical."

"Okay!" Monica throws a hand up. "But why are you acting so *weird* about it?"

DeSean looks at me again, his mouth open.

And now it seems like everyone's waiting for me to say something, but I don't what else to say, so instead I blurt out, "Because I told DeSean yesterday that I wanted to drop out of the show! Okay?"

Mateo peers at me. "You do? Why?"

The room grows quiet. DeSean says, "Because Nikhil thinks that I should be the lead. And he's worried that he can't sing."

But now Monica's eyebrow is arched in my direction, and I have a feeling that the more we talk about this, the less I'm going to be able to hide. "It's not just that I can't sing!" I say. "It's—" I stick my tongue out. "It's that . . . Guuuuuhhhh!" A deep grunting noise comes out of me. It slides up and down inside my chest. "It's that my voice is changing, too! OkaAAEEhy?" And of course, it happens. It cracks.

DeSean eyes me. "Wait, so *that's* what this is about?"

I shake my head. "No! I mean, partly! But it's not *just* that—"

DeSean says, "If that's what this is about, it's not that big of a deal. I mean, mine changed last year. And a bunch of kids in our class are going through it. Mrs. Reed can help you. I'm sure she can."

I press my hands against my cheeks. "I can't tell Mrs. Reed! I can't tell *anyone*! No one can know this is happening!"

"Why?" Monica asks.

"Because!" I try to keep myself from shouting. "*I'm* Raj Reddy! What do you think happens if my voice changes?!"

There's a long silence. Like, really long.

And then Mateo whispers, "Ohhhhh. Right."

Outside, the wind picks up, rustling the trees. There's a clanging noise of pots down the hallway and the muted sounds of DeSean's moms talking in the kitchen.

DeSean shakes his head. "But. How can you hide something like that?"

"I don't know. But I have to! As long as I can, anyway!"

Monica crosses her arms over her chest. "Well."

She shrugs. "If it helps, I haven't noticed it before." Then she looks down at the carpet. "I mean, maybe a little? Now that I think about it. But not like what just happened now."

"I know," I say. "I mean, it doesn't happen all the time. But it's *happening*. Just, really slowly."

"Well, that's good, right?" DeSean flips the chair next to his keyboard around and sits in it backward.

"Yeah, but"—I wrap my hands behind my neck—"I can't risk singing at rehearsals! Otherwise, for sure, everyone's going to know. And I have no idea how I'm going to get through the show! Which is why I told DeSean—on top of how unfair it is that he's not playing the lead—that I want to drop out in the first place! But, like, how can I? I mean, what will people think? It was in the paper! And also"—I look at DeSean, thinking about what he was saying in our snow fort yesterday, and it erupts out of me—"I don't want that stupid woman who wrote that email to think she won, any more than DeSean does!" I feel a tear threatening to push its way out. "So, I don't know what to do!"

I brace myself, half expecting everyone to think I'm losing it.

But, to my surprise, no one does.

Instead, Mateo sits down on the bed next to me. "I don't want that woman to win either."

"I don't think any of us do," Monica agrees. "Ugh. This is *such* a mess!" Then she presses her fist against her forehead and takes a deep breath. "So, let me get this straight. Assuming you *don't* drop out. Which it seems like none of us want you to do." She glances at DeSean, who nods his agreement. Then she squeezes her eyes shut. "We have to find a way to keep you from singing at rehearsals so no one knows what's happening to your voice, but somehow still get you ready to be on stage."

"Um. Yeah," I say.

The four of us sit there. Trying to come up with a simple solution to a complicated problem.

Then Monica snaps her head up.

"What?" I ask doubtfully.

She eyes DeSean's keyboard. "Hey, DeSean? How often does Mrs. Reed make you rehearse with her?"

"Not much." He shrugs. "Why?"

"But like, when you say 'not much,' how little do you mean?"

"I mean, barely at all. Not until a few weeks before

the show, anyway. She knows I practice on my own. Or at voice lessons. So she kind of just lets me do my own thing."

"Okay." Monica looks at my sheet music resting on his keyboard, an idea brewing in her eyes. "Well, if you guys are going to work together anyhow, why don't you just tell her that?" She chews on her lip. "But tell her that you're rehearsing on your own *all* the time! That you both *love* doing it!" She's on her feet now. "I mean, if she knows DeSean's coaching you, she probably won't make you rehearse that much!"

"You really think that would work?" I ask, still not convinced.

"I think it's worth a shot!" she says. "Besides, when we get back from break, she always remembers just how much work she has left to do! She'll probably be relieved to have the extra time!"

Mateo chuckles softly. "She always gets *really* frazzled the closer we get to opening!"

"Okay," I say, trying to piece it all together. "But what about the show itself?"

Monica bites her fingernail. "Well, let's see how things go! Maybe your voice will keep changing really slowly and we won't have to worry about it!

Besides, we can always tweak our plan if we need to! And, remember"—a glint forms in her eye—"it's the eighth-grade musical! It's not like we're at Carnegie Hall! All we have to do is get you through the show!"

We all laugh a little, and I can feel a spark of hope forming in my belly.

DeSean grips the back of his chair. "My voice teacher gave me a bunch of exercises when my voice was changing. Like breathing exercises. That totally helped. And your voice isn't even cracking that bad. I think this could work."

Mateo sticks his hand in front of his chin and waves his fingers at Monica. "Nice plan, Mon! I like it!"

And then, even though it's really their thing, DeSean sticks his hand out in front of his chin, too. And so do I. It feels totally silly. Wriggling our fingers makes all four of us giggle. Uncontrollably. And the longer we do it, the harder we laugh.

Then, out of nowhere, I feel a pillow smack me in the back, and I look up to see Mateo scrambling off the bed.

"Hey!" I say, grabbing the pillow next to me.

But Monica swipes it out of my hands. And the next thing I know, DeSean is yanking on the comforter underneath me. I hop up and grab the other end of it, and now the four of us are having a . . . pillow-comforter fight?

By the time DeSean's moms are knocking on the door, telling us the pie is ready, the room is a total mess.

And as I walk home that night, my belly full and my music stuffed in my backpack, for the first time in a long time, I think maybe, just maybe, everything's going to be okay.

CHAPTER 26

When we get back from winter break, somehow, our plan works.

DeSean and I ask Mrs. Reed to meet with us on stage after school one day. He sits at the piano, and I drop my sheet music down in front of him. I very carefully sing the first few lines, breathing exactly like he taught me at every rehearsal we had over the break. "Nikhil and I got excited about the show, and we decided to practice together over the holiday." DeSean smiles up at her, his fingers dancing along the keys. "So, if you wanted time to, I don't know"—he shrugs—"focus on other things at rehearsals, or whatever, we're totally happy to keep working together. On our own."

"We love working together," I pipe in. "And like I always say . . ." I freeze, realizing I'm not actually sure how to finish my sentence. Then, magically, I spit out, "Teamwork makes the dream work!"

Mrs. Reed rubs her chin, a look of concern in her eyes. Then she opens her binder filled with all the materials for the musical. A couple pages spill out and land on the floor. "Honestly, there *is* a lot to get done! I still have four whole numbers to choreograph!" She presses her fingers against her temples. "If I let you do this, you have to promise to keep checking in and let me know how it's going. Okay?"

"Of course!" We both nod enthusiastically.

She gathers up the papers off the floor and stuffs them back into her binder. Then she mutters, "Why do I put myself through this every year?"

And the truth is, there is a lot to get done. What felt like plenty of time before suddenly seems like a race to the finish. There are backdrops to paint and costumes to piece together, and everything has to be loaded into the school auditorium in just weeks now.

To my surprise, Mr. Cooper, the history teacher, is running crew. And it turns out, when he's not droning on about the Renaissance, he's an entirely different person.

"Who here's ready to paint?" he asks as we all help him unfurl a huge muslin across the floor of the gym. He chuckles to himself as he hands us cans of paint in every color possible. "Did you kids know that I once played the Candlestick in a production of *Beauty and the Beast*? At the Elmhurst Community Theater?"

Monica nudges me and whispers, "He tells this story every year!"

"You won't believe me," he goes on, "but the backdrops were so spectacular, they got a standing ovation every single night!" He hands out paintbrushes. "And so did the Candlestick, if I do say so myself!"

Mateo and I are working on the backdrop for Monica's *Matilda* number when a paint drop lands on my nose.

"Wha?" I look up to see Mateo's paintbrush mid-flick.

I raise an eyebrow and snap my brush back at him. Except instead of landing on him, a gooey drop of purple paint hits the side of Mr. Cooper's cheek.

I'm expecting him to give us a talking-to, but to my surprise, he laughs. By the end of the afternoon, all twenty of us kids—*and* Mr. Cooper—are covered head to toe in paint.

When Mrs. Reed comes in to check on us, she practically yanks out her hair. "Mr. Cooper! The paint is for the *muslin*, not their *bodies*!"

At the studio, Bob continues to offer me hot water, honey, and lozenges before every recording session. And even though he keeps telling me that I sound great, one day he points at his engineering desk. "I'm going to let you in on a little secret, okay, Nikhil?" he says. "If I push this button, it mutes you, and no one in Los Angeles can hear a word you're saying. So, if you need to clear your throat, or sip some water, you just give me the secret signal"—he mimes grabbing his throat like he's choking—"and I'll be ready!"

"Can the secret signal be something a little less . . . *dramatic*?" I ask. "How about"—I point my finger at my throat three times—"just this?"

"I like the way you think, kid," he says. "Let's save the theatrics for the voice acting!"

Between rehearsing for the musical with DeSean, building sets at school, and recording at the studio, I barely have a free minute. But when I do, I have to work on getting ready for Cartoon Con.

For the table read, we'll be performing a shortened version of the script.

Just ten pages.

And honestly, practicing with DeSean seems to be helping my voice. A lot.

I help him out with acting stuff, too. I give him some tips about what auditions are like, and I offer to ask Josh if he knows any casting directors who work on Broadway. Which gets DeSean really excited. He tells me about how he watches the Tony Awards every year, and then he lists the names of all the theaters he hopes to perform in some day.

We both share how we work on scenes. I tell him how I try to imagine the other character—whether it's a giant pink alien or Commander Marks—and really talk to them. How I try to get a reaction out of them. And he tells me how he tries to connect what he's singing about to something that's going on in his own life.

We practice it with his *Dear Evan Hansen* song, and I start to feel . . . emotional.

It reminds me what I love about acting in the first place.

So much so that when I sit on my bed, with those

ten pages in front of me, I remember how I *used* to feel playing Raj Reddy in the studio. When it was just me and the other characters. In outer space. Without any of the pressures of the real world.

One night, I'm deep into my Cartoon Con script when there's a knock on my door.

"Come in!" I say, expecting it to be Mom.

But it's Nana.

He's in a sweater with a scarf wrapped around his neck. He leans on his walking stick, which seems to shake under his hand, and when he looks at me, his eyes seem more sunken than usual.

"I hear you're going to LA?" he asks. "You have to take a day off from school?"

I nod, expecting him to berate me for how much schoolwork I'm going to miss.

He looks down at the carpet. "Well. Good luck."

My lips part in surprise, but before I can say "thank you," he closes my door, and I hear his feet shuffling off down the hall.

My text to Anton says:

I'm coming back to LA soon! For Cartoon Con! Can you come with us?

His says:

OMG CARTOON CON????!!!!! 🚀🚀🚀🚀🚀🚀🚀🚀💥💥
💥💥💥💥💥💥   YEEEEEEESSSSSSSSSSS!!!!!!

Me:

It's gonna be so much fun! I can't wait to see you!!!!!!!

And then, before I know it, Mom and I are telling Streak to be a good boy for Nana and Nani, and we're boarding the plane to Los Angeles.

"No way!" I can hardly contain my excitement when the flight attendant pulls open a curtain and directs us to the front of the plane. "You didn't tell me Josh was flying us first class!"

Mom winks at me. "Beats five days in a Subaru, huh?"

We're cruising over the Grand Canyon when Mom reaches across the seat and takes my hand. "Nikhil?" She clears her throat. "I, um . . ." She looks down at me. "I wanted to talk to you about . . ." She squeezes my hand. "Well, you're growing up, huh?"

I'm not sure where she's headed, so I shrug. "I guess so."

She takes a deep breath. "You know around this age, your body starts to go through some pretty major changes."

"Okay," I say. I feel my cheeks redden—is this going to be one of those *s-e-x* talks? But then I get a sinking feeling in my stomach. Has Mom noticed my voice is changing?

"I mean, are you aware of . . . anything?"

She runs a hand along her throat, and as soon as she does, I'm positive that that's what this is about.

Of course Mom's noticed that it's changing! She's my *mom*! She's probably known for a while.

I throw my head back up against the seat. "Mom, can we please not talk about this *now*?"

She raises her eyebrows. But then she glances at all the other passengers around us and lets go of my hand. "You're right. This probably isn't a good time . . . You're just so busy these days, it seems like there's *never* a good time." She pats my arm. "Anyway. We'll talk about it later."

The whole rest of the flight, all I can think is: Why would she bring this up now?

Josh sends a fancy stretch limo to pick us up at the airport, and when it drops us off at our house, everything looks exactly the way it did the day we left. Our plush white sofas with their oversized furry pillows, the big-screen TV hanging over the stone fireplace in the living room, the carpeted staircase that goes up to my bedroom—nothing's changed.

I tell Mom that I want to work on my script, and then after we order pizza, I yawn as wide as I can. "Whew! I'm beat," I say, not wanting to give her the opportunity to talk about my voice. "Must be all that flying. I'm going to hit the hay."

I think I hear her hovering outside my door, so I stay as still as possible, praying that she'll think I'm asleep.

My phone dings, and I grab for it on my nightstand. I throw the covers over my head, trying to turn the volume off before it can ring again.

It's Anton.

Are you ready, Reddy?!

I write back:

Oh, I'm ready! I'm *Raj Reddy*!

CHAPTER 27

C artoon Con takes over the entire Los Angeles Convention Center.

Anton and I press our faces up against the limousine window as it winds past the sea of fans in the street and pulls up to the enormous glass complex. Our jaws drop when we see the billboard-sized tarp draped over the side of the convention center. It announces *Cartoon Con . . . where your favorite characters come to life!*

Anton grabs my arm. "That's you, Nikhil! You're coming to life!"

I playfully shove him and then fake him out.

"Look! It's Tom Kenny! From *SpongeBob!*"

"Where? Where?" he screams, his head whiplashing back and forth.

"Gotcha!" I say. "Although I bet he's here!"

We pull up to the "Talent Drop-Off Area," and the limo driver lowers the back window. Josh sticks his head out and flashes his convention badge. "I've got Nikhil Shah, star of *Raj Reddy in Outer Space.*"

"Right this way, sir." A security guard opens our door and guides Josh, Mom, Anton, and me toward the entrance.

Josh throws his arm around my shoulder, and I lean into him. It's nice to see him in person after so long. A tinge of guilt creeps into my stomach about all the things I've been hiding from him. But I push it away.

Just get through today, I tell myself. *It's just a few more hours.*

We walk past a set of glass doors and onto the main floor of the convention center. Endless lines of people wait their turns at curtained booths with folding tables set up in front. There are virtual reality booths, booths where actors sign trading cards, booths where you can buy *Star Wars* paraphernalia or vintage *Bugs*

Bunny posters. It's like Disneyland for cartoons.

We have to cut across the floor to get to the hall where we're doing the live table read. When we get there, Josh flashes his badge, again, at another security guard. A line of people has already formed behind a velvet rope. A man at the front recognizes me. He calls out my name, and suddenly phones go flying up in the air. Someone yells, "Are you ready, Reddy?" Anton grimaces, looking more nervous than me. I wave at the crowd, but thankfully, Josh ushers us into the room.

Inside there are rows and rows of chairs sprawled out in front of a stage.

"How many people are going to be here, anyway?" I ask.

"I think about a thousand," Josh says.

Panic flies into my stomach.

"Hey, Nikhil!" Faraja Mwangi is making her way down the aisle toward me. Anton grips my arm. "Whoa! Is that really her?" he gasps. "Commander Marks?"

Faraja's a tall Kenyan American woman with a deep, booming voice and an infectious laugh. She pulls me tight into her. "I have missed running into you at the studio, honey." She presses her cheek up against mine. She hugs Mom, too, and then she shakes Anton's hand.

He grips her fingers so tightly, she has to gently pry her hand away.

"That's quite a handshake you have there," she says.

"Thanks. It's one of my best qualities." Anton nods.

Minutes later, Josh is at the podium on the front corner of the stage, and Faraja, myself, and the rest of the actors are seated at a long table to his left.

The lights glaring down on us make it hard to see, but I spot Anton and Mom smiling at me from the front row. A thousand dark heads fill in the chairs behind them.

I pat my pocket, checking for the lozenges Bob gave me. I lightly hum, just how DeSean taught me.

Josh finishes his speech: "Here to give you a sneak peek of our season finale episode"—he throws his arm toward us—"please welcome the cast of *Raj Reddy in Outer Space!*"

The room bursts into applause.

We lean into our microphones as the audience quiets down. Faraja has the first line.

              COMMANDER REGINA MARKS
    Raj?!! You there?

                  RAJ REDDY
    (whispers frantically into his watch)
    Now? I'm in the middle of science class!

There's a tittering of laughter.

              COMMANDER REGINA MARKS
    What's more important, playing with a
    Bunsen burner or saving the universe?

The laughter grows.

                  RAJ REDDY
    Aw, come on! Tell that to my report
    card!

Now they're laughing even harder. And by the time I'm strapping on my jetpack and crashing through the ceiling of the boys' bathroom on this line—

I hope the Interspace Surveillance Com-
mission is going to pay for that broken
ceiling! My allowance won't cover it!

—we have the audience in the palms of our hands. I can't believe how fun it actually is to perform live. My nerves melt away with each passing line, and the laughter from the audience fuels me. I never get to feel this in the sound booth.

A few pages later, I'm hovering over my chair. It's one of the biggest moments in the script, a showdown between Raj and the alien Crantanica.

RAJ REDDY
(hurling a flaming meteor ball)
Take that, Crantanica! And remember, I
never want to see you on this planet
again!

I'm feeling so confident that I let my voice rip.

And that's when it happens—through the microphone, magnified a zillion times by the towers of speakers on either side of the stage. "I never want to see you on this plAAAaaeennEETAAhhhaTtt again!" My voice skyrockets up to the roof of the exhibition hall and ping-pongs across the walls.

I freeze, my butt half out of my chair.

Everyone in the hall leans forward in their seats.

And then, all at once, they erupt into laughter. Waves and waves of it. But it's joyful laughter.

I hear someone say, "How'd he *do* that? That was awesome!"

I look to Josh, confused. He smiles and mouths, "Keep going! You're doing great!"

I sit back down and pray that my voice will hold up until we get to the end.

CHAPTER 28

As soon as the table read is over, Josh hustles the cast out of the room and guides us down the hall for interviews.

Anton rushes up beside me. "This is going to go down in cartoon history! Did you hear how hard they were laughing?"

"I know, but"—I keep walking fast, trying to keep up with Josh—"did you hear my voice?"

"Mm-hmm." Anton's expression is serious. "But it worked! Didn't it?"

"I wasn't in control of it!" I hiss.

Josh pushes open a set of double doors to reveal a sea of reporters.

With every video camera that's shoved in my face, I cross my fingers that no one will bring up the crack.

One reporter asks, "Raj Reddy's hitting those teenage years, huh?" and holds her microphone out to me to respond. I freeze. But Josh ushers me along to the next interview. "New episode out next week!" he calls out to her. "You've got to see what this kid does in it. He's amazing!"

And then, finally, we're piling into the limousine.

No one mentions a thing about what happened the whole ride home.

But when we drop Josh off at his house, he says, "No need for goodbyes right now. I'll stop by and see you tomorrow before you leave, okay?"

There's a smile behind his words, but he avoids making eye contact with me.

"Okay." I nod, trying to act excited to see him again. But I can't ignore the feeling that he's coming to say more than goodbye. "Can't wait!"

CHAPTER 29

The doorbell rings.

"Nikhil, can you get that?" Mom calls from her room. "I'm just finishing getting dressed! I'll be right there!"

I hesitate at the top of the stairs.

The bell rings again. Then it rings one more time.

I force myself to lower my foot, a dread growing in my stomach with each passing step.

When I open the door, Josh is—once again—smiling too big.

"Hey, buddy!" he says.

Mom comes hurrying down. She leads us into the living room.

Josh sets his blazer next to him on the love seat, and Mom and I sink into the sofa, across from him. The coffee table stretches out between us.

Mom takes my hand. Then she nods at Josh.

I eye the both of them.

"So," Josh says. He smiles even bigger than before, and when he does, I see the slightest tremble in his lower lip. Then he glances around the room and gestures vaguely at the fireplace. "Is that a new painting?"

"Josh," Mom says gently. "Our flight is in a few hours."

"Right. Right." He clears his throat.

I fight every impulse in my body to tear myself off the sofa and run back up to my room.

"I'm really sorry about the timing of this, Nikhil," he says. "But. As I told your mom. I wanted to talk to you about this in person. And now that you're living in Ohio, it seems like I never get to see you anymore."

I brace myself. Is this it? Is this how Josh is going to fire me?

He rubs the palms of his hands along the front of his thighs. "Nikhil . . ." He takes a deep breath. "Where should I start? You're . . . well, I want you to know that you've been such a dream to work with.

You know that, right?" He searches my face.

But I don't respond.

I'm not even sure *how* to respond.

"From the very first day I met you . . . I've been . . . well, I've been so grateful for you. You know, when I created *RROS*, all I had was some ideas. About who these characters would be, and what the show was going to be about."

I pull my lower lip into my mouth and bite down.

"And then you walked into that audition room! From an open call, no less! And you made my hopes come true in a way that I could never have imagined!" His eyes are bright. "I can't thank you enough for that!"

He shifts in the love seat, and then he stares down at his nails.

"It's okay, Josh," Mom says.

"Right." He looks back up at me and exhales. "Nikhil. The thing is. In animation, whenever we cast someone as young as you to play a role, we know that we're taking a chance."

He glances between Mom and me. "What I'm trying to say is . . . Well, I knew your voice would start to change at some point." His words start to come out faster. "And listening back to the last few records, your voice already sounds so much lower than it did when we started. And now that the season is almost over . . ." He presses his fist against his thigh. "Well, when the season ends, I have to recast you with another actor. I'm so sorry, buddy."

I finally respond. Nodding, as if everything he's saying makes complete sense. As if it's not a big deal at all. But inside, I feel like something is crushing me. And my brain is doing everything it can to block all of Josh's words out of my head.

Mom holds my hand a little tighter. "Honey, are you okay?"

But I'm not okay. The tears are already coming. Uncontrollably. And even though I already know the answer to this, I ask, "But is there any way that you can just . . . you know . . . Why can't . . ." I'm having trouble breathing. "I mean, why can't Raj's voice change, too? Just like mine is? Can't you just figure out a way to make it so that I can still play him?"

Josh's lips part, like he's not sure how to answer. Mom hangs her head. She looks so helpless.

"Because, Nikhil," Josh says, "Raj's voice *can't* change. He can't grow older. That's . . . well, that's the beauty of his world. That any kid out there can watch any episode of *RROS*, any day of the week, and they'll always see a snarky, fun-loving twelve-year-old boy trying to juggle middle school while saving the universe. Raj can't grow up." His voice softens. "I hope you understand."

But I don't understand. I don't *want* to understand.

I don't want him to take this away from me. I don't want to stop going to recording sessions. I don't want to stop stepping into the sound booth and disappearing into outer space.

If I'm not Raj Reddy, then who am I?

I jump off the sofa and run up the stairs.

Just as I'm about to close my bedroom door, I hear Mom say, "I don't know if there ever would have been a good time to tell him this. But . . . he's just dealing with so much right now."

"I'm sorry." Josh sounds defeated. "I thought I owed it to him to tell him in person. Was this a mistake?" There's a pause, and then he says, "You know I think of him like a son. Should I go talk to him?"

"I think I should talk to him first," Mom says.

I hear Mom say goodbye to Josh, and I shut my door.

A few minutes later, she knocks softly.

"Come in," I say, and my voice is hoarse.

She wraps her arms around me. "Nikhil, I'm so sorry."

I wipe away my tears. "Have you known that this was going to happen for a long time now?"

She rests her hand on my knee.

"Josh called me a few weeks ago. And the truth is, I've heard the changes in your voice. I have. Your nani has, too." She closes her eyes and takes a deep breath. "But we could tell that you were stressed about it. And I didn't want to say something that would make you more uncomfortable." She turns to face me. "Oh, Nikhil. I might have messed this up. And I'm sorry if I did. But I wasn't sure how to talk to you about it. And when Josh called me, I didn't know if I should talk to you first, or if I should let him tell you himself. And. Well, we both wanted you to have the experience of Cartoon Con—without having to worry that it was . . . that it was ending." She looks intently at me. "I hope you'll believe me when I say that I was just trying to do what I thought was best. For you." She pauses. "That's all I ever want for you."

I nod. And then I say something that surprises me. "Honestly, Mom, I'm glad you know. I'm tired.

I'm really tired of trying to hide the cracking from everybody."

She pulls me close to her. "I had a feeling that might be the case, Nikhil." She squeezes my shoulder. "But can I ask you a question? *Why* do you feel like you have to hide it so much?"

I pick at my comforter. "I don't know. Because I didn't want to lose the cartoon?" I say. Then I let out a big sigh. "And because of the musical."

Mom's brow wrinkles. "How are things going with that?"

I think about how hard DeSean and I have been rehearsing. About how we haven't been honest with Mrs. Reed.

"Nikhil, if your voice is . . . if you're struggling with the musical, you don't have to feel pressured to . . ." She lifts my chin up. "I mean, you don't have to prove anything just because that woman wrote that email. If that's what this is about." Her eyes soften. "And you can always ask for help. I hope you know that. From your teachers. From me. From all of us."

I feel something unfurl inside me. Like a knot is letting go.

"I know, Mom," I say. "I know."

* * *

On our drive to the airport, I pull out my phone and open up the *RROS* Instagram account.

I look at the comments from all the people who love Raj Reddy so much.

Then I turn my phone off and slide it back into my pocket.

CHAPTER 30

It's dark when we land in Ohio. Nani is waiting at the airport, standing by her car, waving at us.

Mom tosses our bags into the trunk. "How's Dad?" she asks as she pulls the passenger door shut behind her.

"He's all right," Nani answers, turning the car on.

But as we drive past the barren cornfields, I catch Nani's eyes in the rearview mirror.

They look worried.

I hear Nana's thick, gurgling cough before we're even in the front door.

"When did this happen? We were only gone a few

days!" Mom wheels her luggage in. She heads straight for Nana's bedroom. I pick up Streak and follow her.

When Mom cracks open the bedroom door, Nana raises his head from where he's sleeping and looks at us. I gently wave at him, and he nods, his eyes still half-closed.

"Let him sleep," Nani says. "I made an appointment at the doctor's tomorrow."

That night, I hear his cough echoing down the hall.

At rehearsals the next day, we're working with the lights and scenery for the first time.

The auditorium is pitch-black except for a single lamp glowing on the wooden tabletop Mrs. Reed has set up over two rows of the audience, as a tech table. The lamp casts a dim light along the side of her face. She flips a page in her binder. Then she speaks into a handheld microphone. Her voice fills the theater. "Mr. Cooper? Are you ready up there? Let's run through a few of the opening cues, and then we'll get the cast on stage!"

There's a shuffling noise and a small crash from the sound booth way above where all us kids are sitting in the auditorium. A few seconds later, a spotlight hits the dark red curtains.

"Cue one!" Mr. Cooper says with a flourish.

"Excellent!" Mrs. Reed peers at the stage through her glasses. "This is where we'll find our Narrator at the top of the show!"

I reach for the arm of my chair, and when I do, I accidentally grab DeSean's hand.

"You okay?" he asks.

"Mm-hmm." I nod.

But I'm not. In just a few minutes, I'm going to have to get up there and sing. In front of everyone.

"Okay." Mrs. Reed leans into her microphone again. "Let's see cues two and three, please!"

"Coming up!"

The curtains go flying open, but one of them gets stuck before it makes it halfway across the stage. A backdrop starts to lower in. One edge is angled three feet higher than the other, and the whole thing bounces to a halt before it hits the ground.

"Sorry!" Mr. Cooper bellows. He sticks his head out of the booth. Then he belly laughs. "You know, this reminds me of the time I was playing the Phantom in *The Phantom of the Opera* at the Oakwood Community Theater! In the middle of my big number, my mask fell off! It was just hanging off the side of my cheek! I had no idea until I heard the whole audience laughing! Can you imagine?"

"That sounds like a great story, Mr. Cooper," Mrs. Reed deadpans. "But can we focus on these cues, please?"

There's a whirring noise, and the curtains close. When they open again, they stick in the exact same place, but this time, the backdrop comes crashing onto the stage with a thud. "What in the name of Dionysus?" Mr. Cooper pops his head back out. "I am *so* sorry!"

Mrs. Reed claps her palm against her head. "Is the music working, at least?"

There's a popping noise in the speakers, and then the low rumble of a drumroll begins. The first few notes of the opening number start to play.

It's the intro. To my song.

"Delightful!" Mrs. Reed exclaims. "At least we have the music! Nikhil, are you out there? Let's at least rehearse the top of this song, and Mr. Cooper and I will address this backdrop issue after you kids are dismissed."

DeSean whispers, "You've got this. It's going to be great!"

But I'm glued to my seat.

"Hurry up, sweetie!" Mrs. Reed scans the audience. "We have a lot left to do!"

I trudge down the aisle. I climb up the four short steps to the lip of the stage. I take the microphone out of the stand hidden just behind the curtain.

The drumroll starts again.

I take a deep breath.

The first note plays.

I open my mouth to sing.

But I stop. I just can't make myself do it.

Instead, I wave my arms at the booth.

The music keeps playing.

"Can you cut the music, Mr. Cooper? Please?" I ask into the mic.

I hear whispering among the rest of the cast.

"What'd I do now?" Mr. Cooper shouts. "Is this the wrong song?"

But I don't answer him. Instead, I drop the mic by my side and look at Mrs. Reed. "Can I talk to you?"

She walks up to the stage, and I kneel down. "What's wrong?" she asks.

Behind her, I see kids leaning forward in their seats. "Can we talk in private?"

There's a confusion in her eyes, but she nods.

"Can DeSean come with us, too?" I ask.

The three of us head into the dressing room, and Mrs. Reed flips on the lights. The bulbs on the makeup mirrors are bright. Too bright. I can see myself reflected a thousand times, like I'm in a fun-house mirror.

We pull three chairs into a circle.

I take a breath, and then I try to keep my voice as calm as I can. "Mrs. Reed, I shouldn't be the lead of this musical."

She cocks her head at me.

"Can I explain?" I ask.

"Okay." She nods.

"DeSean has the best voice in our class. Everybody knows that. You basically told him so the first day of school. He's the one who should be playing this part."

Mrs. Reed's jaw drops.

"Nikhil?" DeSean tugs on my sleeve. "What are you doing?"

"I'm sorry," I say to him. "I just . . . I think we've been doing this all wrong." I sit up a little taller and face Mrs. Reed. "The whole reason DeSean and I have been rehearsing on our own is because . . ." I hesitate. "Well, I can't sing all these songs. And I feel like you know that! I mean—" I force myself to keep going. "I'm pretty sure you only cast me in this role in the first place because I'm Raj Reddy!"

Mrs. Reed starts to protest, but I have more to say. "I mean . . . you named your cat Commander Marks, didn't you?"

DeSean's eyebrows fly up his forehead. "Wait! Seriously?"

Her face flushes. "I already explained this to Nikhil! They have *very* similar personalities!"

I press on. "But the truth is, I'm not *just* Raj Reddy! I'm also a regular middle schooler!" My eyes start to well up unexpectedly. "And I'm scared to be on that stage. I'm scared to sing." I blink back the tears. "And I can't believe you haven't figured this out yet!" It comes flying out of me. "But my voice is changing. It's cracking and sliding all over the place, and nOOOooeew . . ." My voice flips, yet again making its point right on cue. "Well, I'm not even Raj Reddy anymore, okay? I got fired! *Because* of my voice!"

DeSean turns to me, a look of surprise on his face. "I'm so sorry, Nikhil."

"*You* shouldn't have to be sorry! You're the one who should be playing this part in the first place!"

I hadn't planned on all this coming out now. And I hadn't planned on spilling our plan to Mrs. Reed without talking to DeSean first.

But it's too late to take it back.

I bury my head in my hands.

Minutes seem to go by.

Quiet.

I think I hear Mrs. Reed swallow.

"I'm sorry about your show, too, Nikhil," she says gently. "That must be hard. I'm sure it hurts. A lot." She reaches for a box of Kleenex on the dressing room table. "But please don't think of it as being fired." She hands one to me. "I'm sure that's not what it is. Sometimes, things just change. That's all."

She waits for me to wipe my tears. "And it doesn't take away from all the wonderful things you did with that role. All the people you made laugh. That will last forever. You should know that."

She thinks for a moment. "And I knew the two of you were up to something, rehearsing on your own. I should have intervened. Of course I should have! But . . . well, I was proud that you both wanted to help each other. I wanted you to do what you needed to do, to feel comfortable on that stage."

She smooths the front of her pants. "Now, about the casting . . ."

While Mrs. Reed gathers her thoughts, DeSean leans forward in his chair. "Mrs. Reed, why *didn't* you give me the lead? Is Nikhil right? I mean . . ." He pauses. "Did you really just give it to him because he's Raj Reddy?"

She looks caught off guard. And there's a long silence.

"Well," she says quietly. "If I'm being totally honest . . ." She turns to me. "Nikhil, you're very funny, and you're such a great actor. And I think you're doing a terrific job acting this part! But"—a pained expression forms on her face—"I guess I also thought . . . that the other kids would be excited to have a TV star as the lead. That *really* wasn't fair of me." She takes a breath. "And, DeSean." She looks him right in the eyes. "I owe you a *big* apology. Of course you deserve to be playing this part. I know how hard you've worked, and all the promises I made. And believe me, there are Broadway singers who'd kill to have a voice like yours! I thought giving you several solos would be a good way to showcase your talent, but the truth is . . . well, I wrote all these

Narrator songs with you in mind!" She exhales. "I'm so, *so* sorry. Can the two of you ever—" She stops herself. "No. I'm not going to ask you to forgive me without finding a way to make this right first."

She runs a hand through her hair. "We open in three weeks. So we don't have much time, but I promise you . . . *both* of you . . . I will find a way to make this better. Okay?"

I look over at DeSean. I want to make sure it's all right with him.

"That sounds good, Mrs. Reed," he says.

A look of relief crosses her face. "Can I just say one more thing? And then I want to hear *your* ideas on how we can fix this. Nikhil, I know your voice is changing. Of course I do. This isn't my first time at the rodeo! I've been teaching middle school long enough to know that boys' voices change. A couple of cracks in a middle school musical is really not that big of a deal. And I promise you"—she smiles at me—"you *will* be okay." She rubs her hands together. "All righty then. More importantly! How do we fix this situation? So that you both get to do what you do best! And we can still put on our show?" There's a hint of panic in her voice. "Keeping in mind that we only have a few weeks left!"

But before we can even try to come up with an answer, there's a knock on the door.

Principal Dawson pokes his head in. His face looks ashen, and there's an urgency in his voice when he asks, "Mrs. Reed, can I have a word, please?"

The two of them step into the doorway. We hear sharp whispers, and DeSean and I glance at each other.

We lean forward, trying to hear their conversation.

"I tried to reason with her," Principal Dawson says. "But she wouldn't listen. I think we have to be prepared for the worst."

"Well, how close can they get?" Mrs. Reed's words tumble on top of his.

DeSean mutters to me, "Do you think this is about that woman? Who wrote the email?"

I strain to hear more.

"I don't think past the parking lot," Principal Dawson says. "The rest of the school is private property. But regardless, I'll make sure we have security."

I lean in even more, and the foot of my chair squeaks against the floor.

Mrs. Reed looks back at us.

"What are you guys talking about?" DeSean asks.

She shakes her head. "Nothing to worry about.

But we're going to end rehearsal early today, all right?"

"We need to make some phone calls," Principal Dawson says. "To all your parents."

CHAPTER 31

Constance Shaffer is planning to protest the musical.

She somehow managed to gather a group of people who are just as hateful as her. They're planning to take over our school parking lot the night of the show. Who knows what else they'll try to do.

Principal Dawson isn't sure how many of them there are. But there must be a lot. Because she told him to expect the local news to show up.

All because I'm gay.

It sends a ripple through the school. Kids are talking about it in the hallways. Principal Dawson calls a meeting with the parents to tell them about the steps he's taking and to assure them of our safety. DeSean's mom and momma reach out to Mom, and the three of them carpool to attend it.

At our next rehearsal, Mrs. Reed calls all twenty of us together on stage. Not to sing. Or dance. Or work on our lines.

Instead, we all sit in a circle.

I find a spot next to DeSean. Monica sinks down on the other side of him, and Mateo slides in beside me. His backpack is draped across his lap, his finger tracing lines across it as though he's drawing in his sketchbook.

Mrs. Reed asks us to hold hands.

"I want you all to know that I'm trying to figure out a few changes to the musical. And I'll let you know what those are as soon as possible. But today, I want to address what's happening with these people who are trying to threaten our show." She makes eye contact with each one of us. "You should all know that the theater has a long history of inspiring protests. It's because theater *says* something. It makes a statement. Whether it's the subject matter of the play, or the casting of the actors. From Greek tragedy to musicals about the Vietnam War to *Hamilton* on

Broadway, theater makes people think. It challenges them. It pushes for change. And sometimes people don't like that! It makes them angry! And that's a good thing. That's exactly why we do it in the first place!"

Her passion fires everyone up, and as she continues to speak, I realize that I no longer want to run away. I'm done with disappearing.

"So they can try whatever they want out there, but it'll only make our show that much better!"

I grip DeSean's and Mateo's hands a little tighter, and they both squeeze mine back.

CHAPTER 32

"I just think, if Mrs. Reed's going to change the show anyway, then why don't we *really* change it!" Mateo's whispering urgently.

The four of us are hiding in the stacks of the library, trying to keep our voices down.

Mr. Cooper had been too distracted to teach today. It was pretty clear that he was anxious about everything going on with the show. He'd dropped his whiteboard marker, like, three times, and kept calling kids by the wrong names. Finally, he'd leaned over his desk. "For the rest of class, why don't you all just go to the library?" Then he'd tried to act stern. "But I want you to each write a short report!

On . . . well, anything you want! But write about something!"

While the rest of our classmates have their heads buried in their notebooks—trying to figure out what the assignment is—Mateo rounded up the four of us, and we snuck off to the shelves.

I slide out one of the books behind me and peek at the checkout desk, to make sure Mrs. Rahmani—our librarian—can't hear us. She's squinting at her old desktop computer.

"What do you mean, *really* change the show?" DeSean asks.

Monica's leaned up against a row of books, her arms crossed over her chest. "Yeah. Like, what kind of changes are you talking about?"

"I'm not sure!" Mateo shoves his hands into the pockets of his faded jeans. "All I know is that Mrs. Reed said theater makes a statement! That it makes people angry! And I don't get how singing the songs we've been rehearsing *makes a statement!*"

Monica uncrosses her arms and slowly starts pacing. I back up to make room for her.

"I mean, I just keep thinking, if that woman's going to be there, in the parking lot, making all that trouble"—Mateo shakes his head—"then wouldn't it be cool if what we do on stage"—he scrunches up his face—"could . . . I don't know, *piss* her off, too?"

My eyes widen at his language. A few kids look up from the tables in the center of the library, and I raise a finger to my lips, glancing at Mrs. Rahmani.

Monica stops pacing. Then she says, "I think Mateo's onto something."

We all face her.

"Have any of you considered that there's a fundamental problem with our show, anyway? And I'm not talking about all this stuff with the Narrator."

"What kind of problem?" I scratch my elbow.

Her nostrils flare ever so slightly. "I mean. Listen. I love singing the Matilda song. I do. And DeSean's an *amazing* Evan Hansen. But doesn't it bother you all that none of these characters look like us?"

"What do you mean by that?" DeSean squeezes his brows together.

"I mean"—Monica throws a hand up—"Matilda's not Korean! Evan isn't Black!"

"Oh." DeSean sighs. "Right. I know where you're going with this. But . . ." He tilts his chin her way. "Here's the thing. Maybe Evan wasn't Black *originally*. But he's Black when *I* sing him! And other

Black actors have played him. On Broadway! Which is actually really important!"

Frustration is written on Monica's face. "I know. I guess what I mean is . . . Why do *we* always have to change the characters to fit *us*? Why can't we ever play characters who were written Korean in the first place? You know? Or Black? Or Mexican? Or . . ." She looks at me. "I mean, that's one of the things that was so cool about Raj Reddy!"

I hold her gaze, remembering how I felt, knowing that someone had written a cartoon with a lead Indian role.

DeSean shakes his head. "Well, there aren't that many musicals about Korean kids. Or Black kids!" Then he adds, "I mean, of course there are some! But there aren't *enough*! And a lot of them aren't great for, you know, middle school." He looks at her. "Besides, am I *only* allowed to do Black shows?"

I peer through the shelf again, but Mrs. Rahmani's still poring over whatever it is she's fixated on at her computer.

"No! Of course not!" Monica says. She gets quiet. "I just wish it weren't so complicated! Or that there was something we could do to make it better."

I stare down at my sneakers. "Even if we could," I say, "what does that have to do with what Mateo's asking?"

"Because I think what Mateo's trying to say"—she goes to stand by him—"is if this woman is protesting *us*—then maybe a way to make a statement would be if our show had more of *us* in it. Like, if there was a way we could, I don't know, talk about what it's like to . . . be gay! Or Korean! Or Mexican! You know, share *our* experiences? Instead of singing about Kristoff and a snowman!" Then she mumbles, "Even though Kristoff is *totally* adorable."

A grin spreads across Mateo's face. He points at Monica. "Thank you, Mon! That's *exactly* what I was trying to say! You just . . . said it better."

The four of us chuckle quietly. Then DeSean runs his finger along the spine of the book next to him. "Let's say we *do* try to do this. To change up the show. Where would we even find songs about *our* experiences?"

Monica looks off to the side. "I don't know." Then she shrugs. "Maybe, if no one else is writing them, we just have to write them ourselves!"

"Wait, really?" I ask. "Write our own show?"

Mateo crouches down, both his arms extended.

"Does it only have to be songs? What about something about skateboarding?"

Suddenly, about five books on the bookshelf get yanked out of place. We all spin around. Mrs. Rahmani's face pops up. "So, I guess this means the four of you already completed your report? For Mr. Cooper?"

"Uh-huh. Yup," we mumble, grabbing our bags. "Totally done."

We're halfway down the stacks when Mateo turns around, stopping us.

"Wait. Can we really do this?" he asks. "I mean, I know we don't know *exactly* what we want to do yet. But can we at least promise that we'll talk to Mrs. Reed about it?"

I remember the first time I met Mateo, how he'd been standing behind Monica, not saying much.

It's cool to see him so riled up.

We're all nodding, lost in our thoughts, when the bell rings. DeSean and Monica start heading toward the door, but Mateo reaches for my arm and leads me back into the stacks.

"Everything okay?" I ask.

"I wanted to tell you something," he says, and I see him swallow.

"Yeah?"

His voice gets breathy. "I, um. I did it. I . . ." His eyes grow wet. "I told my parents I'm gay."

I feel something burst in my chest. "You did? No way! How'd it go?"

"It went really well." He smiles. "They were so cool about it." He's standing so close to me, I can almost feel how warm he is. "I just wanted to say thank you for that."

"What?" I ask, shaking my head. "Why would you thank *me* for that?"

"Because," he says. Then he reaches up on his tippy-toes and plants the softest kiss on my cheek.

I freeze. I don't move for what feels like forever. But inside, I feel like I'm flying all the way to the moon and back.

CHAPTER 33

I get a ride home from school with DeSean that day. When I walk in the front door, Nani is sitting in her chair, reading the news on her iPad, but the rest of the house is completely quiet.

"Is Mom in the basement?" I ask.

"Mm-hmm." Nani smiles at me. "I think she had some work to finish."

I scoop up Streak and head downstairs.

I expect to find Mom hunched over her desk, but instead she's sitting on the sofa with a cup of tea.

"Mom?" I ask.

She pats the cushion next to her. "Come, sit. How was school? How are your friends?"

"Good." My heart races, just thinking about Mateo. Why did I have to freeze like that? Why didn't I kiss him back?

I'm afraid Mom's going to read my thoughts, so I quickly change subjects. "We talked about the musical. A lot. We have some ideas we want to ask Mrs. Reed about."

Streak nestles his head against Mom's leg. "How are you feeling about all that?" I hear the concern in her voice. "Are you holding up okay? Everyone's being supportive?" Then she adds, "And Mrs. Reed is still figuring out a way to help you with your voice?"

"Mm-hmm." I shrug. "I'm glad I talked to her."

Mom squeezes my arm. "That makes me really happy, Nikhil."

There are bags under Mom's eyes, and I can tell that she's more tired than usual. So I ask, "How are you, Mom?"

She rests her hand on my cheek. "I'm okay." Then she takes a deep breath. "I'm just . . . Well, you know, your nana's going through a rough patch."

"I know." I nod. Then I ask, "Is he really bad?"

Mom blows into the curls of steam rising above her teacup. "I hope he'll improve, but . . ." She trails off. "Well, he's not doing so good right now." She shifts on the sofa, turning a little more toward me. "I brought him lunch in his room today, and he was asking me all sorts of questions about you. He wanted to know if you're upset about the cartoon ending. If you're scared of the protest . . ."

I run my hand along the hair on Streak's back. "That's nice of him."

Even though I never told Mom that I overheard her and Nana all those months ago, I have a feeling she knows. Because, more quietly, she says, "I think he's really trying to understand . . ."

I look up at her. "Did you ever talk to him . . . about . . . what happened with you and Dad?"

She nods, slowly. "We did. A little." She sets her tea on the coffee table. "And it was really good." There's a distant look in Mom's eyes. "You know, Nikhil, for all the mistakes Nana made, there are things I wish I had done better, too. I didn't really know how to stand up for myself when I was younger. Sometimes, it seemed easier to just . . . I don't know . . . run away." She lets out a small laugh. "I mean, I moved us all the way to Los Angeles, didn't I?"

I raise my shoulder ever so slightly, not sure how to answer.

"Anyway." She gently waves a hand in the air.

"I'm really proud of you, Nikhil. Watching how you're handling everything. You're a very courageous young man."

She smiles. "And I think you teach me how to be more courageous."

I shake my head. "No way, Mom," I say. "You're the one who taught me everything I know."

When I head back upstairs, Nani's still in the living room, but I notice the light spilling out from under the door to Nana and Nani's bedroom.

I drop Streak off in my room, and then I walk down the hall.

I knock quietly on Nana's door.

"Avo," he says in Gujarati.

When I open the door, Nana has the covers pulled up to his chest.

There's a dining room chair by his bed where Mom and Nani sit when they bring him his lunch. Or his medicines.

I lower myself into it, right next to him.

Neither of us says anything, but I can tell that he's happy that I'm there.

Then Nana takes his hand out from under the covers and holds it out to me.

"I'm sorry, Nikhil. For what I've done," he says.

I take his hand in mine, doing my best to not start crying.

"I love you, beta," he says, very quietly.

"I love you, too, Nana."

After I leave Nana's room, I think about how lucky I feel to have so much support right now. In the face of this woman who's trying to take me down.

And for some reason, it makes me remember what DeSean's moms said. About how different things were for them in middle school.

I realize that what Mateo wants to do with the musical is exactly right.

We *should* figure out a way to show everyone who we are.

And then, an idea hits me. I run into my room and grab my phone. I message the three of them:

If that woman's going to protest us, why can't we protest
her right back?

CHAPTER 34

Mrs. Reed's jaw drops. "I've already been rearranging things! Divvying up the songs! Seeing if I could maybe make Nikhil and DeSean co-Narrators! Now you want to rewrite the whole musical?"

"Well, not *all* of it! But can we at least change *some* of it?" Mateo pleads.

The four of us are in Mrs. Reed's classroom, gathered around her desk. We should be at lunch right now. But there's no time to waste. We had to talk to her before rehearsal today.

"How much of it?" she asks, squeezing her temples. "You know there's just a little over two weeks left now, right?"

"We just want to make the show more about *us*. That's all!" Monica leans forward. "And not just the four of us, but all of us kids in the musical."

Mrs. Reed is silent for what feels like a full minute. Then a strange, exasperated cry comes out of her mouth. "Um, okay?"

"Also." DeSean nods at me. Then we both say—in unison—just like we practiced, "We want to have a counterprotest. In the parking lot."

"A counter—? I'm sorry. What now?"

"A rally!" I say.

Mrs. Reed slowly sinks into her chair, thinking.

The four of us eye one another. Waiting. Then, Mateo says, "Mrs. Reed, we just want to use the theater to make a statement. That's all."

I see something shift in her.

"We want to do it on stage . . ." Monica sets us up.

And DeSean and I bring it in for the finish. "And we want to do it to their faces. At our very own rally."

We all hold our breath.

Then Mrs. Reed flicks the comedy and tragedy pendant dangling from her glasses. It twirls around and around. "Come with me."

The four of us walk down the hall to Principal Dawson's office.

We wait outside his door while Mrs. Reed and he talk.

After just a few short minutes, the doorknob turns and Principal Dawson asks us to come in.

There's a glimmer in his eye as he starts. "Mrs. Reed told me what the four of you want to do. And I'm really proud of you kids." He pauses. "I'd like to make this happen. I would. But my concern is that we don't have enough time. A rally—in the parking lot of our school—would require a ton of logistics . . ."

"What kind of logistics?" I ask.

"Well, we'd need volunteers! To set things up! And we'd have to figure out how to redirect the parking with all the people who'd be coming to the musical. We'd need a PA system—"

"What if we all promise to help?" Monica asks.

"And *perform* in the musical that night?" Principal Dawson looks skeptical.

"We could ask our parents to pitch in!" DeSean offers.

"And I bet I could get the faculty on board," Mrs. Reed thinks out loud. "I'm sure a lot of them would love to volunteer." An excitement grows behind her words. "I can ask some of them to speak, too!"

Principal Dawson grins at our enthusiasm. "Well, I suppose if it's all hands on deck . . . then who says we can't pull this together in two weeks?"

The next several days fly by. Mr. and Mrs. Salas, the Kims, Mom and DeSean's moms, and almost every single parent with a kid in the musical—and parents *without* kids in the musical, too—sign up to volunteer at the rally. Even Nani does!

Principal Dawson arranges to bring in more security. Mrs. Rahmani and Mrs. Gonzalez call all over town trying to find rental chairs, microphones, speakers—everything we could possibly need.

Mr. Cooper helps us make posters in his class. Mom even comes in one day to offer us some graphic design tips. We use markers, glitter, and poster board to make signs supporting people of all identities and backgrounds.

Rehearsals are intense. We all agree to stay even later than normal.

Mrs. Reed sits all twenty of us down on the stage and asks, "So. If you could tell the audience something about yourself—anything at all—what's the story you'd want to tell?" She passes out blank sheets of notebook paper and pencils. "And *how* would you want to tell it?"

But we're all stumped. Staring at the blank lines on the pages in front of us.

And even if we could answer her, how will we ever put a whole new show together in the little time we have left?

After rehearsal, she pulls me aside. "Nikhil, what if we turn your opening number into a monologue? Not *my* words, but something that *you* write? Something funny, ideally, that would draw in the whole audience."

"Um. Okay. But what should it be about?" I ask.

"What do you *want* it to be about?" she asks back.

And if that weren't hard enough, she adds, "I also think it's important that you say something at the rally, okay? Principal Dawson is going to speak. And some of the other faculty. But I think people will really want to hear from you."

"Right. Like a speech?" I ask.

"Mm-hmm."

I try to push down the fear. "Are you sure?" I ask.

"I'm one hundred percent sure," she says.

* * *

Every night, I pace around my room, literally banging my head against the wall, praying that ideas will come.

For the show *and* for the speech.

Finally, one night, I decide to video-call Anton.

"Hey!" I say, relieved when he answers. His face breaks into a huge grin, and I realize that we haven't really spoken since Cartoon Con.

I called to pick his brain. But instead it feels nice to just catch up.

"The bathrooms still smell like farts," he jokes when I ask him about school. Then he smirks. "Oh! And I'm building a solar-powered roller coaster for the science fair."

"Whoa. Really? That's cool!"

"It's *totally* cool. It's going to be massive! With an upside-down loop and everything!" His cheeks start to redden. "And guess who I'm building it with?"

"I dunno." I shrug. "Who?"

"Melissa"—he adds a question mark to her last name—"Roper?"

I wait for him to say more, not sure if that's a good thing.

"Turns out, she's a total science nerd," he says proudly. "The solar panels were *her* idea!" Sweat starts to trickle down the front of his brow. "Nikhil, you're never going to believe this. But . . . I think she might *like* me!"

I high-five him through the phone.

He asks me about the musical, and when I tell him about the rally his eyes grow wide. "I wish I could be there," he says. "That actually sounds cooler than Cartoon Con."

"I wish you could be here, too." I smile. "Oh . . . and um. I think someone here likes *me*, too! And . . . he's. Well, he's really cute." Now I feel sweaty.

I tell him about Mateo's sketchbook and how he loves to skateboard. And how he always makes us all laugh when we least expect it. Even though he's also kinda shy. Which, I guess, is like me.

But I leave out the kiss. I don't want to share that with anyone just yet.

And then, it's two days before the musical, and I still don't have a single word written.

My blank laptop stares at me.

I stare back at it. Angry.

I type a letter.

I erase it.

I type another.

And then, finally, I slam it shut.

I jump off my bed. I tiptoe quietly past Nana's room. I head to the kitchen for a snack. Maybe that'll help?

"Everything okay, Nikhil?" Nani asks, looking up from her book at the dining table.

I yank out the chair next to her. I drop my head against the table and moan, letting it all out. "No! I have no idea what to write!"

She closes her book, waiting for me to pull myself together.

"Do you want to hear what I used to tell my students?"

I nod, desperate.

She clears her throat, and when she speaks, I can almost imagine her standing at the front of a classroom. "Whatever you're writing. Whether it's something funny. Or serious. It must always come from the same place. Your *truth*."

I wait for her to go on. But she doesn't say anything more. "That's it?" I ask.

"That's it," she says.

I pry my head up off the table. "But what does that mean? My truth?"

"Only you can figure that out." She puts her hand

on mine. "But I always told my students, the most important thing is to listen to your heart."

After everyone else goes to bed, I sit at my desk.

I force myself to open my laptop back up.

I hear both Mrs. Reed and Nani in my head.

"What's the story I want to tell?" I ask myself. "What's my truth?"

Ugh. What does that even mean?

I close my eyes.

I think about everything that's been happening lately. All the stuff that I've been dealing with.

Is that my truth?

But so much of it just feels hard, that it doesn't seem like it would make a very funny monologue.

I squeeze my eyes shut even tighter.

I think about how my voice sounds when it cracks.

Like a dying cat.

I chuckle.

A tiny bit of excitement starts to bubble up somewhere deep inside me. It pushes into my chest and runs down my arms. It spills into my fingertips.

I press my fingers against the keyboard, and I start typing.

CHAPTER 35

There's a cool spring breeze the evening of the musical.

But inside Mom's car, the air feels thick, and I have to remind myself to breathe.

We still don't know what Constance and her mob of angry parents are going to try tonight when they show up. Or how ugly it might get.

I clutch my backpack against my chest.

I stayed up late memorizing everything I wrote. My speech. My monologue. All of it. But stuffed inside my bag are printed-out copies of everything. Just in case.

Mom reaches across the gearshift. "How are you doing?"

I want to tell her I'm great. That all my nerves have gone away.

But the truth is, I'm the most nervous I've ever been.

And I'm excited.

"I'm okay," I say.

Nani reaches forward from the back seat and massages my neck. I swivel around to hold her hand and try not to think about the empty spot next to her.

Earlier in the afternoon, I'd knocked on Nana's door. He was sitting up in bed, two pillows propped behind his back. Mom was in the chair beside him, helping him with his lunch.

"Come in!" he'd said.

I sat on the edge of the mattress, next to the lump that his legs were making. "Nana?" I asked tentatively. "Do you think you want to come with us today?"

Mom quietly watched him, his hand shaking on the tray of food in his lap.

"Of course I'm coming!" he'd said, and his voice was surprisingly strong.

But when it was time to walk out the door, Nana was even more shaky than before. And his walking stick was wobbling under his weight. He made it from the bedroom to the living room and then said, "Let me just sit for one minute! Then we can go."

"Dad, I think it's better if you stay here," Mom said. "Nikhil will tell you all about it when we get home. Okay?"

I feel Nani squeeze my neck again, and I blink, letting it go.

"Don't worry," she says. "We'll take lots of pictures for him. I promise."

Mom turns into the school parking lot. It's still early, and there are only a few other cars here. I see Monica getting a garment bag out of the trunk of her parents' sedan. Her mom and dad take turns giving her hugs.

"We'll be out here setting up!" Mom kisses my cheek. "But if you need anything, just call me, okay?" She squeezes my hand. "I love you, Nikhil."

DeSean's moms come over and there are even more hugs.

"You're not going to believe how many folding chairs Principal Dawson ordered!" Tonya points at the far end of the lot, one hand stuffed into the pocket of her thin, puffy coat. We all turn to see three pallets of chairs lined up next to a set of risers that are waiting to be arranged into a makeshift outdoor stage.

"We've got our work cut out for us!" Kristy laughs. "But it's nothing we women haven't done before, right?" She winks at Nani. To my surprise, Nani pushes the sleeves of her jacket up and says, "I'm ready! Just tell me where to start!"

I say my goodbyes and then call out to Monica, "Wait up!"

She hangs back on the sidewalk.

"Is your costume in there?" I ask, looking at her garment bag, wishing I could see inside. I realize that we haven't even had time to do a full dress rehearsal.

"Mm-hmm." She nods. "I designed it myself."

Backstage, nerves are running high. But, like me, everyone seems to be feeling a mixture of anxiety *and* excitement. A few kids are hanging up their stuff. Others are unraveling their posters for the rally. Large wooden sticks and superglue are being passed around to attach to the signs. From the bathroom, I hear the echo of DeSean's voice gliding up and down scales.

"Hey, everybody!" I say, letting the door shut behind me. Everyone turns my way, and there's a smattering of applause. "What's that for?"

Monica nudges me, her arms still wrapped around her garment bag. "What do you think it's for?" she asks. "It's to let you know we've all got your back."

My eyes well up, and I try to play it off. "What? No! Tonight's about all of us!"

More kids arrive. When Mateo comes in, he loosely high-fives me, and our fingertips linger. I want to let my fingers curl down and hold his. I think maybe we both do. But we quickly pull apart when Mrs. Reed bursts in, followed by Mr. Cooper. He's carrying a large bouquet of roses.

"Okay! Quick, quick, quick! Everyone find a seat!" She claps, gathering us all together. "We have so much to do before the rally!" DeSean comes out of the bathroom and pulls up a chair next to me. We clasp each other's forearms.

"First off—and most importantly—it's opening night!" Mrs. Reed motions to Mr. Cooper. He takes the rubber band off the flower bouquet and starts handing each of us a rose.

"No, no!" she gasps. "I just meant you can set those down. We'll give those to the kids *after* the show."

Mr. Cooper whispers, "But don't you always give out flowers *before* the show?"

"No!" She shakes her head. "That's bad luck! Everyone in the theater knows that!"

His face falls. "Really? Well, that explains it! That must have been what happened when I was playing Peter Pan with the Brookside Players! One minute I was flying in the air, and the next thing I know I'm crashing into Tinker Bell! It must have been those darn flowers!"

All twenty of us suppress our giggles, and for a second it relieves the tension in the air. Even Mrs. Reed laughs.

Then she turns back to us. "As I was saying, the flowers are for after the show! But I want to tell you what I love about flowers on opening night, okay?" She pauses dramatically. "Flowers are beautiful! But they only last for a little while. Even so, long after their beauty has wilted away, you'll still remember how they made you feel.

"Which is exactly the same as theater! What we do on that stage will all be over as soon as the curtain comes down." She leans forward. "But the way you make people *feel* tonight. The beauty you create. Well, they'll remember that forever!"

She stands up and sticks her hand out. All twenty of us pile ours on top of hers. She looks each of us right in the eye. "That's the power of theater!"

Emotion wells up in her voice. "I want you all to

know that no group of people, no matter how much trouble they try to cause, can ever take that away from you! Tonight, before our show, we are going to march back to the parking lot and meet those protesters head-on. And some of you have prepared some things to say. And I am so proud of you for that. And we are all going to stand together. And then, no matter what happens out there, at seven thirty, we are coming back into this theater and putting on the show of our lives. Because the show *always* goes on! Now let's do this!"

Twenty pairs of hands go flying into the air, and Mr. Cooper high-fives each of us as we file out of the dressing room.

We quickly warm up on stage, rolling up and down our spines, and stretching our faces. All twenty of us stand in a circle and play a lightning-round game of Zip-Zap-Zop. Mr. Cooper runs through the first few cues, and then, just before six thirty, we all grab our signs and make our way back to the parking lot.

All twenty of us stand together on the sidewalk. We take in the transformation that's happened in the parking lot.

Principal Dawson is standing on the now-completed makeshift stage all the way on the far end of the lot. A podium has been placed on top of the risers, and stacks of speakers flank each side. When he steps up to the podium and taps the microphone, the speakers spring to life.

In front of the stage are what look like hundreds of folding chairs, perfectly lined up in rows.

My stomach dips. What if nobody shows up? What if Constance and her group outnumber us?

Next to the stage I see three parked news vans, their satellite dishes pointing up at the sky.

My phone dings, and I slide it out of my pocket. It's Anton, texting.

> Nikhil, break a leg tonight. I just wanted to tell you that you've been my best friend for as long as I can remember, and I couldn't be prouder to know you.

I feel like I'm going to be a mess. So, I snap a selfie, being sure to get the news vans with their satellite dishes in the shot. I text it to Anton.

> Can you imagine the aliens we could track with these things?!

Then I add:

I can't wait to tell you all about tonight. You're my best friend, too.

Monica leans her head against my shoulder. "Did you see the news vans?" she asks.

"Uh-huh."

She points toward the other end of the lot. "Did you see the police, too?" she asks. I follow her gaze to where four police cruisers are pulling in the parking lot gate.

My chest tightens, and Monica reaches for my hand. She squeezes it.

What if something bad actually happens tonight? What if someone tries to do something violent?

Cars start to pull in. Then a few more.

A pickup truck pulls into a parking spot, and Big Bob gets out. He waves at me, and I mouth, "Thank you for coming!" I'm so happy he's here.

Because the stage takes up half the lot, cars are now having to park on the grass outside the school. I guess people are actually turning up. Maybe even more than we expected.

In the front row of the audience, I see DeSean talking with his moms. Mateo's taking a selfie with

Mr. and Mrs. Salas, and Monica's hugging her parents.

But I don't see Mom. Or Nani.

I scan the lot.

When I finally spot them, way off by the front gate, I suddenly feel overwhelmed.

In between Mom and Nani is Nana. He moves slowly, like each step takes a fair amount of work. He's clutching his walking stick in one hand, and his other arm is around Mom's shoulder.

I tear off toward them. "Nana! You came?"

"He wouldn't stop calling me," Mom says, smiling. "So we had to go back home to get him."

"Isn't it too cold out here for him?" I ask. "Did you have to park far away? He shouldn't walk so much!"

"It's okay, Nikhil," Nani says. "This is where he wants to be."

I look up at Nana.

And then, I lower myself down and touch his feet.

He rests his hand on the back of my head.

"You always have my blessings, beta," he says. "Always."

CHAPTER 36

Principal Dawson is at the podium, and myself, the rest of the cast, Mrs. Reed, and Mr. Cooper are lined up in a semicircle on the stage behind him.

From where I'm standing, I have a clear view over the heads of the hundreds of people sitting in the audience. I can see all the way out to the parking lot gates. The sky is darkening, and the streetlights towering over the cars are beginning to glow.

And that's when I spot them. A sea of posterboards undulating out in the street and heading our way. There's a low chanting that gets louder and louder the closer they get. "Not at our school! No way! No how!"

It's so surreal that all these people could be this angry—at me. Just for being who I am.

I feel an impulse to run away. But another voice is telling me to be strong.

As they come through the gates, the police step out of their vehicles and rest their hands on their batons.

In the folding chairs, everyone stands up and slowly turns around to face them. We start chanting back, raising our own posters higher. "No hate! Only love! No hate! Only love!"

The protesters are almost up to the back row of the audience now, and the lights on one of the police cruisers turn on. The car's siren makes a short noise, like a warning signal. There are maybe a hundred of them. And at the very front is a woman who I just know is Constance Shaffer.

She's yelling into her megaphone, one arm raised over her head.

She's white, with straight brown hair to her shoulders. She's wearing a light blue windbreaker and dark jeans.

She looks so ordinary. Like she could be anyone's mom.

My stomach churns. Maybe that's what's so scary about her.

"Not at our school! No way! No how!" she shouts into her megaphone. All her followers chant it back.

Principal Dawson leans into the mic. "We will never tolerate hate here! Not at *our* school!" Everyone in the audience starts clapping and stomping their feet, drowning out Constance and her mob. They make a point of turning their backs on her, spinning around to face Principal Dawson. "Sycamore is a place where all identities are celebrated!" He raises his voice. "Where every student is treated as an equal!"

Constance shouts, "Take the gay back to LA!" and in the front row I see Mom curl her hand into a fist. Nani rubs her back.

Someone in the very back of the audience hops up onto his chair and gets in one of the protesters' faces. He raises his fist, and the police come running in.

I reach for DeSean. He's holding his chin high, but his eyes are filled with fear.

"Hang on now!" Principal Dawson calls. "We don't have to meet them on their terms! We can stand our ground peacefully!"

There's more clapping from the audience. Then Principal Dawson says, "Maybe those angry parents could learn a lesson from these amazing students behind me! What do you think?"

A whoop goes up in the crowd. Principal Dawson looks over his shoulder at us. Then he leans into the mic. "Mrs. Reed? Would you care to join me up here at this podium?"

Nobody's paying attention to Constance anymore. All eyes are on the stage.

Mrs. Reed feigns surprise at Principal Dawson's invitation, but then she unzips a garment bag stowed at her feet. She pulls out a sequined, rainbow-colored tuxedo jacket. She swings it around over her head, to make sure everyone can see it. The crowd erupts into applause as she wiggles her way into it. She literally glitters as she takes the mic. "Art has always been about expressing your *what*?" she yells. And our entire cast cheers back, "Your *self*!"

"After this rally tonight, who's excited to see the best show that Sycamore Middle has ever put on?"

Now the audience is screaming uncontrollably. It feels like we're at a concert.

Constance and her group of parents keep trying to make themselves heard, but Mrs. Reed talks right over them. She motions at DeSean, Mateo, Monica, and me, beckoning for us to join her at the podium. "These four kids brought us together tonight, and they have something to say." She spins her wrist up over her head and bows our way. "You kids inspire me every single day! Let's all give them a big round of applause!"

The four of us take a step forward.

I've walked up to a microphone a million times, it seems. Almost always, it's to slip on a pair of headphones and shut out the real world.

But tonight, there are no headphones. I can hear everything around me.

All these people are clapping and stomping their feet. For us. For me.

We take another step forward, and I realize just how nervous I am. I'm shaking.

But I feel something else, too.

I feel so alive right now.

The four of us grab for each other's hands.

From somewhere off to the side, I hear a news reporter say, "Taking the stage now is Nikhil Shah, the star of the popular animated series *Raj Reddy in Outer Space*."

But when I lean into the mic, I'm not Raj Reddy.

"I'm Nikhil Shah," I say. I catch Mom's eyes; she's beaming up at me. "And with me are my friends DeSean Hill, Monica Kim, and Mateo Salas."

The audience erupts in applause. Someone yells, "We love you kids!"

"Um. Thank you all for being here," I start. I can hear Constance's group still chanting their ugly words, but I focus on the sound of my own voice.

"My mom and I moved to Ohio at the beginning of the school year," I say. "But I didn't really know what moving would mean." The printed-out copy of my speech is folded into my back pocket, but I don't need it. "As some of you know, for a long time, I've played a character on an animated series," I say, and someone yells, "Are you ready, Reddy?"

There are a few chuckles in the audience, but I press on. "But that's not who I really am."

Constance stops to watch me. Across all the heads, I somehow make eye contact with her, and for a second, everything slows down. Like time is standing still.

Then I let it go and come back to all the people who are here for me tonight.

"I'm also just a thirteen-year-old kid. And I was scared to move here. Because I was nervous about making new friends. And meeting a family I didn't really know." I look down at Mom, and I see her wiping away a tear. "But. I'm glad we came. Because I wouldn't trade in the friends I've made here for anything in the world. Or my teachers. And"—I see Nani take Nana's hand in the front row—"I'm happy I got to know my family. I love them." I take a breath. "I guess what I'm trying to say is, I'm just a kid. Who happens to be gay."

Someone yells, "No hate! Only love!"

And it grows, and grows, and grows, until the whole audience is up on their feet chanting.

Principal Dawson says a few more words, and so do some of the other faculty. And then at seven thirty p.m. sharp, Mrs. Reed takes the microphone. "Well, folks! It's half an hour until showtime! I need all my actors backstage!" She twirls around in her sequined jacket. "The show starts promptly at eight!"

As I'm stepping off the risers, Mom runs up to me and pulls me into her. "You were wonderful, Nikhil! I'm so proud of you!" The wind is picking up a little, and it blows her hair into her face. She brushes it away. "I'm going to take Nana home, okay? I think the show will be too long for him to sit through. But Nani and I'll come back to see you on stage."

I look for Nana in the audience, but everyone's standing up and gathering their things, and it's too hard to see past them. "Will you tell him thank you for coming?"

"Of course I will!"

As our cast hurries down the sidewalk, we have to file right past Constance and her group of parents. They're still loud, but it's obvious that they're losing steam. Some of them even look down when we walk by, and I wonder if they're too embarrassed to yell right in our faces.

I see a man, with a can of spray paint in his hand, being lowered into a police cruiser, and as we turn the corner, I can make out the words "Not at our" sprayed across the brick wall of the school.

And then, finally, we're in the dressing rooms. The rally and the protesters are far away, and now it's showtime.

I'm smoothing down my hair when DeSean leans over my shoulder, his face right next to mine in the mirror.

"We did it, huh?" He smiles.

"Totally," I say. Then I take a sharp inhale. "DeSean, I'm *so* nervous!"

"Me, too!" He laughs. "But. Now that we got

through that rally, I think we can pretty much do anything, don't you?"

Monica and Mateo join us, and now all four of our faces fill the mirror. We're breathless, excited. And we can't stop smiling.

Mrs. Reed's voice crackles through the backstage speakers. "Actors, this is your places call. Actors to places, please!"

All twenty of us are crowded in the wings when the house lights go down. A hush falls over the audience, and a recording of Mrs. Reed's voice pipes through the speakers. "Welcome one—and welcome *all*—to the Sycamore Middle School Spring Revue, *HEAR US ROAR!*"

Our show isn't totally different than it was before. There was no way we could change everything in just two weeks.

But there's way more of *us* in it.

And we're planning to be loud about it.

The stage lights cut to black.

"Go, Nikhil! Go! That's your cue!" I feel twenty pairs of hands searching for me in the darkness, pushing me out onto the stage.

It's pin-drop quiet. I walk toward the glowing X

taped down front and center.

I place one foot on either side of it, and almost instantly, a spotlight springs to life.

I stare at the audience, frozen. Dark outlines of heads and shoulders fill every seat.

That familiar panic starts to seize me. But I push it away. I'm too excited to be scared.

"So?" I raise my hands up to my shoulders and cock my head. "What'd you all think of that pre-show?"

To my relief, the audience bursts into applause.

A few minutes later, I'm walking along the edge of the stage with a microphone in my hand. "Have any of you ever had your voice crack in front of a thousand people?!" I slide my voice up as high as it'll go, making it crack. "I sounded like a dying cat! No website called 'Puberty Is Your Friend' can ever prepare you for that!"

People are leaning out of their seats, they're laughing so hard.

"And besides, that's not a friend I want!" I deadpan. "No thanks! Hard pass!"

My eyes have adjusted to the lights now, and from where I'm standing I can see Nani's face, laughing, in the front row, right next to Mom.

I talk about playing Raj but give it a comedic twist. "Wait, this character's brown, and he *doesn't* have an accent? Are you *sure* he's Indian?"

By the time I finish, the audience is up on their feet, clapping and hollering.

And with each act that follows, they only get more riled up.

We perform some of the songs we originally rehearsed with Mrs. Reed. DeSean sings "You Will Be Found" from *Dear Evan Hansen*, and there's not a dry eye in the house. And the whole audience stomps their feet along to Monica's Matilda.

But we surprise them, too. With all the new things we've been working on the last two weeks.

Monica and five girls take the stage in costumes that they each designed, inspired by some of the world's biggest K-pop stars. The fast-paced beats of Blackpink pipe in through the speakers. The girls lock arms. Six sets of shoulders fly into the air. Then they arm-wave—like an electric current is running through their bodies. They spin out across the stage, knees hiked up, hands over their heads, and from just offstage, DeSean records the whole thing for Monica's cousins in Chicago.

The audience is clapping along when the music

shifts and Chicano Batman comes on.

"Let's go, let's go, let's go!" I whisper in the wings, and seven of us grunt as we push out a giant wooden skate box—that Mr. Cooper helped us build—onstage. And then Mateo's riding his skateboard all across it—crouched down low, his fingertips spread out like wings—twirling his board beneath him and landing on both feet every time.

I smile so hard. And my smile grows even bigger when he gets a standing ovation.

And then finally, we're at the last number.

Mrs. Reed and DeSean walk out. There's just a piano on stage now. Under a single spotlight.

She sits at the bench, her hands poised over the keys. He nods at her, and she starts playing.

Our entire cast crowds in the wings to watch him.

His feet are planted, and he's looking up at the back of the auditorium, just like he did at auditions. In the front row, I can see his moms, on the edge of their seats, holding hands.

He starts singing the lyrics he wrote.

He sings about how, someday soon, there's going to be a new face on Broadway. That New York better get ready. He tells the audience that when he gets there, he's going to ride an elevator to the top of the

Empire State Building and look out over all the lights of Times Square.

One day, he says, his name will be on a marquee.

When he sings, "Ready or not, Broadway here I come!" the pace of the music picks up, and Mr. Cooper lays in a bass track underneath it. The spotlights start spinning around above the stage, and I see Mr. Cooper waving his arms back and forth in the booth.

DeSean gets to the last verse, and we all run out on stage to join him.

All twenty of us hold hands. DeSean and I are front and center, Monica and Mateo on either side of us. We sing the last words in unison, "Ready or not! Here us ROAR!"

My voice cracks so hard, and I know I'm singing all the wrong notes.

But it doesn't matter. I'm so happy, I could cry.

In the dressing room, we jump up and down and hug each other. We take selfies as we peel out of our sweaty costumes and wash our faces.

When everyone starts to leave, I hang back a second. DeSean fist-bumps me. "Ready? Let's go find our moms!"

"I'll be there in a second, okay?"

And then, everyone's gone, and it's just me under all the lights.

I look at myself in the mirror.

I'm glowing, my skin flushed from all the excitement.

I smile at myself. I feel . . .

I feel proud. Courageous.

The dressing room door creaks open, and Mateo pops his head in.

"Coming?" he asks.

"Yeah," I say.

I walk over to where he's standing. His hands are stuffed into the pockets of his hoodie. Butterflies start fluttering inside my stomach.

I lean in, and I kiss him on the cheek.

CHAPTER 37

The backdrops come down, the costumes get put away, and in what feels like the blink of an eye, the stage looks exactly the way it did at first rehearsal.

But for weeks, the entire school can't stop talking about the show. Or the rally.

"Can I get a quote for the newspaper?" Kyle asks, but this time he's talking to all four of us. He looks at DeSean. "I have so many questions! Like, how'd you come up with the lyrics to that song you wrote?" DeSean seems slightly embarrassed, but once he starts talking, he can't seem to stop.

Josh sends flowers to the house. The note says, *Dear Nikhil, I heard about your rally. I'm so proud of you! We all are. We miss you. Love, Josh.*

There are no more emails from Constance Shaffer. Or, if there are, nobody seems to care.

And for a few weeks, even Nana's health seems to improve.

Mom plays a recording of the show for him, and we all laugh when he sits up and says, "Nikhil! You need to teach me some of those dance moves! Next year, I want to be on that stage with all of you!"

One afternoon, Nani takes down a Gujarati book from her bookshelf. "It's about Gandhi." She smiles. "Maybe you and your nana can read it together?"

I nod.

So, every evening, after I finish my homework, I take the book to Nana and sit beside him in his bed. He squints through his glasses, reading it out loud to me and translating it into English. But sometimes he gets frustrated and Nani comes to help him. The words sound like poetry in her mouth.

One night after dinner, Mom's working in the basement and Nani's in the kitchen when I finish my homework and head to Nana's bedroom.

But when I get there, he's already asleep.

The book is open on his chest, and his head is tilted back.

So far back, it doesn't look normal.

"Nana?" I ask.

I walk over to him.

I put my hand on his face.

It's cold.

It's *too* cold.

I scream, "MOM!" Fear courses through my whole body. I tear down the hall, still screaming. "Mom, come here! Now!"

Nani flies in from the kitchen. "What happened, Nikhil? What happened?"

I hear Mom taking the stairs two at a time. I clutch her arm. "Hurry! Something's wrong with Nana!"

The three of us race to his door. When Nani sees his body, she runs to the side of the bed and rubs her hands across his chest.

Mom lowers her hand over Nana's mouth. "Nikhil! Go to the basement. Fast! Get my phone!"

I grab Mom's phone and run back to her, fighting back my tears as I watch her dial 9-1-1.

When the ambulance pulls into our driveway, the

siren is so loud that I cover my ears.

And then suddenly, there are strangers in our house. Strangers with walkie-talkies and badges. Their hands are all over Nana's body. And when they speak, their voices are cold. Like they could be talking about anyone.

They don't even know he's my nana. Or how much we've been through—and how much we still have left to talk about.

"There are no vital signs, ma'am," one of them says to Mom. "I'm sorry for your loss."

Tears are running down my face. Nani's knees give out, and I do my best to hold her up.

When the paramedics leave, we have to wait for the car from the funeral home. Mom, Nani, and I stay in Nana's room, a sheet pulled over his head. A police officer sits on the sofa in our living room.

The funeral home attendants speak in hushed tones when they get here. They tell us how sorry they are. Then they pick Nana up off the bed and lay him on a stretcher. They ask if we'd like to have a minute alone with him, one last time.

"Can I?" I ask.

"Alone?" Mom asks. "Or do you want me to be with you?"

"Alone."

And then it's just Nana and me in his bedroom.

I shut the door.

It's scarier than I thought.

But I walk across the carpet and stand by his stretcher.

I gently peel the sheet back.

His face looks so different than it did this afternoon. His jaw is slack, and all his wrinkles have smoothed away.

He's so still.

I'm not ready for him to go.

My voice catches when I kiss his forehead. And then the sobs come out hard and heavy. My voice is ragged when I whisper, "Goodbye, Nana."

My hand shakes as I pull the sheet back up over his head.

I must be exhausted, because I sleep in late the next morning.

When I finally get out of bed, Mom and Nani are at the dining room table. They've already showered, and Mom's in her white kurta. Nani's wearing a white sari. She motions for me to join them, and I pull up a chair next to her. She slides a tattered spiral notebook across the table to Mom. "Everyone's numbers are written in here," she says. "We should let them all know."

I sit there, listening, while Mom and Nani go down the list. They call Ramesh and Hansa Patel and the Shah family and all the families that Nana and Nani have known for so many years.

For the next several days, leading up to the funeral, our house is filled with visitors.

Hansa Auntie brings a framed photograph of Nana and a garland of flowers. She sets the picture on the mantel next to the Ganesh statue, and Nani drapes the flowers around Nana's face.

Nani's friends hug Mom. "We can't believe how long it's been since we've seen you!" they say. Then they take my face in their hands. "So this is the young man we've heard so much about!"

They tell stories about when Nana and Nani first moved here.

Some of the stories are funny. Really funny.

And every time we laugh, it makes missing Nana hurt a little bit less.

But still, every time I walk by his bedroom, or see the book that we were reading—which now sits on the desk in my room—I wish I could have just one more day with him.

CHAPTER 38

My graduation gown is made out of this shiny blue material. It's all billowy, like a parachute, and I'm tangled up in it. My arm is in the wrong armhole, and the opening for my head is nowhere to be found. I can't see a thing.

And my phone will not stop ringing.

"I'm coming!" I shout into the mess of blue silk. Streak is barking at my legs, trying to grab the hem of my gown in his mouth.

My head pops out of the top. I'm still one arm short, but at least I can grab my phone. It's Anton, video-calling me.

"Hey!" I say. I wriggle my arm inside the gown,

finally snaking it out of the right hole. "You're up early!"

"I know! I was just too excited!" he says. He's already wearing a tie, and his red hair is combed flat against his head. His lips are covered in green frosting. "Can you believe we survived the eighth grade?"

"What's the green stuff?" I ask.

"Oops!" He rubs his hand back and forth across his mouth. Then he leans into the phone. "My mom made a cake. I'm having a graduation party. Just a few friends."

"Oh yeah?" I ask. "Who's coming?"

But before he can answer, I see Mrs. Feldman walking in behind him. "Anton! Did you *already* mess up my icing? It's only nine a.m.!"

"Welp!" His finger hovers over the phone. "Gotta go. I just wanted to say congratulations."

"Congratulations!" I manage to get in right before he disappears.

Mom snaps a million photos of Nani and me in front of the house. Then, Nani takes a billion more with Mom and me. "Are these okay?" Nani hands me the phone for approval, and even though a lot of the shots are off-center, they're pretty good. With the sun shining so brightly, the photos are crystal clear. I zoom in on my face, and I'm pretty sure I see the faintest hint of a few hairs right above my upper lip.

"Whoa," I whisper to myself.

The school parking lot is a sea of kids in blue gowns making their way toward the gymnasium. The Sycamore prairie dog is shimmying and backflipping across the marquee. As we pull up, I see Monica, Mateo, and DeSean already talking together on the sidewalk. I race across the parking lot to meet them while Mom and Nani mingle with their parents.

"Group selfie!" Mateo cries, and the four of us crowd in behind his phone. I'm throwing a peace sign when I see someone I recognize getting out of a car.

He's in a shiny suit and pointy dress shoes, and he looks way too fancy for an eighth-grade graduation.

"Josh!" I run over to him.

I haven't seen him since Los Angeles, and for a moment we both just stand there, staring at each other. Then I throw my arms around his waist. "I didn't know you were coming!"

"I wouldn't have missed this for the world!" he says. He takes a step backward. "Look at you in that gown! Someone cleans up pretty nice, huh?"

I laugh.

He shields his eyes from the sun. "Hey, Nikhil . . . I'm sorry about, well, the way everything went down . . ."

"It's okay," I say.

He extends his hand, and I reach mine out to shake his.

Mom comes over with Nani, and there's a round of introductions. Then she says, "I'm glad you came, Josh!"

He hits the Unlock button on his keys and reaches into the back seat of his rental car. He pulls out a coffee-table-sized printed album. "Everyone at the network wanted you to have this, Nikhil. We made it for you."

The cover says "To a Kid Who's Out of This World!" I open it to the first page. It's a picture of my very first day in the sound booth at *Raj Reddy in Outer Space*.

"No way!" My jaw drops. "Look how young I am!"

I keep turning. There are candid shots of all the people who work at the recording studio and even some from backstage at the Kids' Cartoon Awards.

I'm only a few pages in when Josh takes the book out of my hands. "Oh, wait, you've got to see this."

He flips toward the end.

The last several pages are copies of fan letters, all addressed to the network.

"We thought you'd get a kick out of these," Josh says.

I skim through a few, but one in particular catches my eye.

It's a drawing. A stick figure that looks like it could be Raj, outlined in brown crayon, staring up at a yellow star. It looks like it was drawn by someone really young, and scratched in below are the words *My name's Raj, too! I'm going to be on a cartoon like you one day!*

"Pretty cool, huh?" Josh puts a hand on my shoulder.

"Really cool." I smile.

The four of us are heading to the gymnasium when Josh quietly says, "So, Deepa, are you planning to stay in Ohio for a while? Or have you given any thought about coming back to LA?"

"We haven't made any decisions yet." Mom reaches for Nani's hand. Then she jokingly adds, "Why? What's the big rush?"

Josh grins. "No rush! No rush! But I'd love to

have Nikhil come by the recording studio at some point! There are a couple producers I want to introduce him to who are big fans of his work. And it'd be great to test his voice out, once it starts settling in."

"*Test* my voice out?" I ask warily. "What does that mean?"

Josh shrugs. "Well, it's not going to crack forever! And once it stops, I want to work with you again! We should find some new characters for you to play. Speaking of which"—he looks at me pointedly—"I heard somebody wrote a hilarious monologue for the school musical! Have you ever thought about writing something for yourself?" He raises an eyebrow. "Maybe you and I should think about creating a show together!"

"Are you kidding right now?" I try to contain my excitement.

"No!" Josh says. "I'm actually not!" Then he laughs. "I mean, I'm not sure if the Writers Guild lets thirteen-year-olds in, but who knows, maybe you could be the first!"

I'm totally speechless. Just past Josh's shoulder, I see Nani smiling in her flower-print dress.

"If you need a writing coach," she says, "you know where to find me."

The gymnasium is already packed when the four of us walk in. Mom, Nani, and Josh look for open chairs on the gym floor, and I head to the bleachers. About eight rows up, Monica's waving me over, pointing at the empty space between DeSean and her. Mateo's sitting right next to her, on the other side.

A dozen kids have to stand up or slide their feet out of the way as I make my way across the aisle to them.

When I finally do, Monica quickly scoots across the bleacher so that she's next to DeSean, and I plop down in the open spot beside her. "I thought maybe you'd want to sit by Mateo," she whispers.

I try as hard as I can not to blush when I mumble back, "Thanks."

Then she says, even more quietly, "Plus." She swallows. "I kinda want to sit next to DeSean."

Mateo and I both grin. Hard.

Principal Dawson steps up to the podium. "It might be your last day as Prairie Dogs"—he leans into the mic—"but I want you to remember that you will always have a home here at Sycamore. You've earned it!"

There's a round of applause, and then he invites

Mrs. Reed to read out the names while he hands us our diplomas. She's wearing a blue gown like the rest of us, but when she steps up to the podium, she tilts her head down. On the top of her cap are comedy and tragedy masks, outlined in rhinestones.

The entire audience chuckles.

As she starts to call us up one by one, I roll my tassel between my thumb and my forefinger.

I remember how Mrs. Reed told us that the musical would only last for a short while. And then everything we did on that stage would disappear.

I think about the book that Josh made for me. My episodes of *RROS* will keep on airing for a long time, maybe even years.

Both of those things have the power to affect people, far into the future.

"Nik-hee-uul Sha-ahh!" Mrs. Reed singsongs my name.

My classmates high-five me as I head up to the stage. The way I feel right now—I think I'll remember this forever.

CHAPTER 39

There are a lot of hugs after the graduation ceremony.

And then there's a giant sheet cake with blue icing in the gym, and one of those towering punch-bowl fountains. The four of us are sticking our paper cups under it, trying not to let the fruity red juice splash all over us, when DeSean asks, "Should we make plans to hang out tomorrow?"

"Can we hang out *every* day?" Monica answers, peering over her cup.

"I'd be good with that," Mateo says, looking at me, and I can tell that I'm not the only one nervous about having to say goodbye.

"I'd be good with that, too," I say.

But a few hours later Mom, Nani, and I are in the parking lot, leaned over Josh's GPS, making sure he knows how to get back to the airport. And then, we're driving home.

We head to our rooms to change. I wriggle out of my gown and peel off my dress shoes. I throw on some flip-flops and take Streak out to the backyard.

It's warm outside, and it smells like summer. Like freshly cut grass.

Mom opens the sliding glass door, and we both sit on the patio steps, our bare feet brushing the blades of grass below us.

"Is Nani coming?" I ask.

"She wanted to make some pakoras." Mom rests a hand on my back. "She'll be out soon." Then she says, "So, I guess we have some thinking to do, huh? About heading back to LA. Or . . . staying in Ohio. For a while anyway."

I feel a pit opening up in my stomach. "What about Nani?" I ask. "I mean, should we stay here for her?"

Mom looks at me. "I think she'd be happy if we stayed, but I don't think she *needs* us to, if that's what you're asking." She smiles. "Your nani is a very strong woman."

"I know," I say. "But . . . wouldn't she be all alone here without us?"

"I don't think so." Mom shakes her head. "You saw how many friends she has here. And I think she'll probably see them even more now."

"Hmm." I stroke the tips of the grass with my toes. "And how do you feel?"

She sits up a little taller and sucks in her breath. "Oh, boy. Well, I don't know, to be honest. I guess . . ." She furrows her brow. "On the one hand, I didn't realize how nice it was going to feel to be here. I'm glad that we came. I'm glad that Nana and I made peace with each other. And that the two of you got so close. And I'm happy that Nani and I have gotten to spend so much time together."

"I'm glad that we came, too," I say. It comes out so easily.

"But," Mom goes on, "do I miss my life in LA? Yeah. Do I miss my friends? Of course. So . . ." She traces a line on the palm of her hand with her finger. "I guess . . . I don't know. What about you? How are you feeling?"

I pick up a broken twig and toss it across the backyard. Streak runs after it.

Next year is the ninth grade. I would love to

start high school with DeSean and Monica. And, of course, Mateo. My heart races just thinking about him. I can only imagine all the things the four of us could do. Together.

But then, Anton comes into my mind. I miss him. A lot. And what about what Josh said? About a new cartoon? And meeting producers? And maybe even *writing* something?

"Nikhil, you still here?" Mom asks. She rubs the back of my neck. "We don't have to decide today, okay? We can think about it."

I nod. "Okay."

But then I say, "I don't know what we should do, Mom. I don't. But I know that I want to stay here for the summer, at least! And I want to make it the best summer ever. Before anything changes again, I want to hang with DeSean and Monica, and spend time with"—I feel my face turning red—"Mateo! And I want Nani to teach me some Gujarati so I can finish reading our book! So, I don't know what we do next, Mom. But right now, can we just stay here? For a little bit longer?"

"That sounds like a good plan to me, Nikhil." She nods. "That sounds like a really good plan."

Behind us, the sliding door opens, and Nani

comes out with a tray of steaming pakoras. She sits with us, and we laugh and we talk while we break the pakoras in half, waiting for them to cool down.

We stay outside so long that the sky starts to grow darker, and the first few stars begin to shine above the horizon.

I look out at them, and I squint until they turn into a sea of glitter.

There's so much ahead of me. So many adventures.

But for now, it feels good to be here. Right here.

With both my feet on the ground.

ACKNOWLEDGMENTS

A few thank-yous I wish I could scream from the mountaintops.

Jessica Regel, my agent at Helm Literary, thank you for believing in me. Your grace and support allow me to call myself an author. To my team at A3 Artists Agency—Richard Fisher, Sharon Paz, Todd Eisner, Andy Patman, Sally Willcox, April Perroni—and to my managers, Colton Gramm and Jai Khanna at Brillstein Entertainment Partners, thank you for always standing by me.

To everyone at Balzer + Bray / HarperCollins, I am eternally grateful for the tireless work you've put into making this book a reality. Donna Bray, Suzanne Murphy, Caitlin Johnson, David DeWitt, Amy Ryan, Mark Rifkin, Kathryn Silsand, Laura Harshberger, Vaishali

Nayak, Sammy Brown, Andrea Pappenheimer, Kerry Moynagh, Kathy Faber, Patty Rosati, Mimi Rankin, Katie Dutton, and Caitlin Garing, thank you.

To my editor, Alessandra Balzer, your endless care, thoughtfulness, and ability to help me dig deeper and be more truthful make me a better artist. I love working with you! It has been a gift to write another book under your discerning eye.

Nabi H. Ali, you breathed life into this cover illustration! I love it so much. I literally can't stop staring at it.

There were a few early readers whose input meant so much: Evan Kennedy, Nat Razi, Jada Johnson, Alejandra Oliva, Lily Choi, I'm so grateful for your time and careful consideration.

Veera Hiranandani, Hena Khan, Kyle Lukoff, Jasmine Warga, and John Schu, I am in awe of each of you—both as people and as authors—and your early support and words of love mean a great deal to me.

Middle school Maulik was profoundly influenced by my own drama teacher, Kathi Grau. Thank you for helping me find my voice. And to David Lyle Solomon, Katie Champlin, and Kelsey Madges—middle school teachers who are shaping the minds of young people today—thank you for the time you spent with me as I crafted this story.

Rashi DeStefano, Sue Jean Kim, Mindy Kordash-Shim, Cyrus Hicks, and Maksim Knapp, thank you for helping me fill in some all-important details.

I'm grateful to have a large, beautiful family who surrounds me with so much love. A few of them bear singling out in this particular process. My cousin, Beej. The care you put into your thoughts and our honest conversations around culture were so helpful.

My sister, Sona. You've been there through every up and down and remind me of my own courage when I need it. Thank you for reading early drafts and for the sage advice. I'm so grateful you're my sister.

To my mom—there is a line in this book where Nikhil tells his mother, "You're the one who taught me everything I know." This is really me speaking directly to you. Thank you for teaching me the great strength that is found in being one's self and on the path of truth. You've shown me this by example. I'm beyond grateful.

And to my husband, Ryan. You are my constant. My grounding force when things feel like they're spinning out of orbit. You teach me who I am because you bring out the best parts of myself. Thank you, once again, for giving me the space and support I need to write, and for being a sounding board and a good listener. You make the journey worthwhile.